"The lovers, kissing each other, began again to rear up, positioning themselves for coitus as their watcher turned away, crawling clumsily on all fours, moving in awkward haste across the clearing until he was close to the riverbank. He rose and, stumbling, in panic, began to run. He ran down the riverbank and along the edge of the current, running until the encampment was far out of sight.

"He stopped and looked back. He was alone. It was as though he were the only living thing in this place. He bowed his head and began to sob, in a harsh broken rhythm, the sound oddly loud as it echoed across the moonlit waters of the river. He stood sobbing in that wild place, bereft of all hope, beyond all forgiveness."

Father Laforgue believed he knew all the dangers that awaited him among the Savages. He was wrong. . . .

BRIAN MOORE was born in Belfast and emigrated to Canada in his twenties. Among his many extraordinarily acclaimed novels are *The Lonely Passion of Judith Hearne*, *The Luck of Ginger Coffey*, *Cold Heaven*, *The Color of Blood*, *Lies of Silence*, *No Other Life*, and *The Statement*. He currently lives in Malibu, California, and Nova Scotia, Canada.

OTHER BOOKS BY BRIAN MOORE

The Statement

No Other Life

Lies of Silence

The Color of Blood

Cold Heaven

The Temptation of Eileen Hughes

The Mangan Inheritance

The Doctor's Wife

The Great Victorian Collection

Catholics

The Revolution Script

Fergus

I Am Mary Dunne

The Emperor of Ice Cream

Canada (with the editors of *Life*)

An Answer from Limbo

The Luck of Ginger Coffey

The Feast of Lupereal

The Lonely Passion of Judith Hearne

BLACK ROBE

A NOVEL

BRIAN MOORE

A WILLIAM ABRAHAMS BOOK

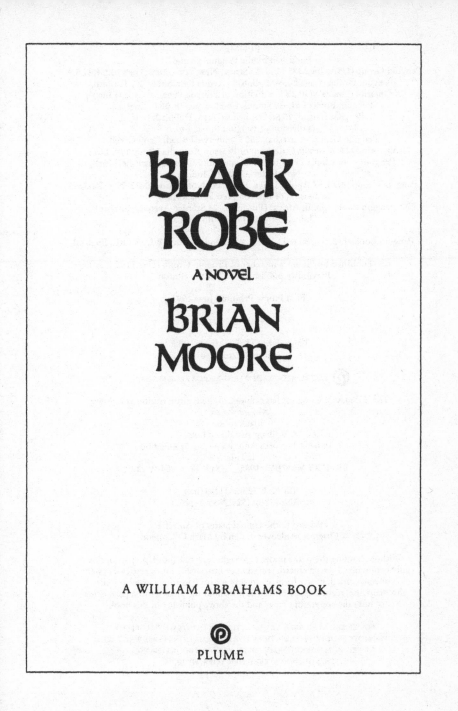

PLUME

PLUME
Published by the Penguin Group
Penguin Group (USA) Inc., 375 Hudson Street, New York, New York 10014, U.S.A.
Penguin Group (Canada), 90 Eglinton Avenue East, Suite 700, Toronto,
Ontario, Canada M4P 2Y3 (a division of Pearson Penguin Canada Inc.)
Penguin Books Ltd., 80 Strand, London WC2R 0RL, England
Penguin Ireland, 25 St. Stephen's Green, Dublin 2, Ireland
(a division of Penguin Books Ltd.)
Penguin Group (Australia), 250 Camberwell Road, Camberwell,
Victoria 3124, Australia (a division of Pearson Australia Group Pty. Ltd.)
Penguin Books India Pvt. Ltd., 11 Community Centre, Panchsheel Park,
New Delhi – 110 017, India
Penguin Group (NZ), 67 Apollo Drive, Rosedale, North Shore 0632, New Zealand
(a division of Pearson New Zealand Ltd.)
Penguin Books (South Africa) (Pty.) Ltd., 24 Sturdee Avenue, Rosebank,
Johannesburg 2196, South Africa

Penguin Books Ltd, Registered Offices: 80 Strand, London WC2R 0RL, England

Published by Plume, a member of Penguin Group (USA) Inc.
Previously published in a Dutton edition.

First Plume Printing, June 1997

24 23 22 21

Ⓟ REGISTERED TRADEMARK—MARCA REGISTRADA

The Library of Congress has catalogued the Dutton edition as follows:
Moore, Brian
Black robe.
"A William Abrahams book."
1. Indians of North America—Canada—Fiction.
I. Title.
PR9199.3.M617B5   1985   813'.54   84–21222

ISBN: 0-525-24311-9 (hc.)
ISBN: 978-0-452-27865-3 (pbk.)

Printed in the United States of America
Original hardcover design by Mark O'Connor

For Jean

AUTHOR'S
NOTE

A few years ago, in Graham Greene's *Collected Essays*, I came upon his discussion of *The Jesuits in North America*, the celebrated work by the American historian Francis Parkman (1823–1893). Greene quotes this passage:

> [Father] Noel Chabanel came later to the mission for he did not reach the Huron country until 1643. He detested the Indian life—the smoke, the vermin, the filthy food, the impossibility of privacy. He could not study by the smoky lodge fires, among the noisy crowd of men and squaws, with their dogs and their restless, screeching children. He had a natural inaptitude to learning the language, and labored

at it for five years with scarcely a sign of progress. The Devil whispered a suggestion in his ear: Let him procure his release from these barren and revolting toils and return to France where congenial and useful employments awaited him. Chabanel refused to listen: and when the temptation still beset him he bound himself by a solemn vow to remain in Canada to the day of his death.

A solemn vow. A voice speaks to us directly from the seventeenth century, the voice of a conscience that, I fear, we no longer possess. I began to read Parkman's great work and discovered that his main source was the *Relations*, the voluminous letters that the Jesuits sent back to their superiors in France. From Parkman I moved on to the *Relations* themselves, and in their deeply moving reports discovered an unknown and unpredictable world. For, unlike the English, French, and Dutch traders and explorers, the Jesuits came to North America not for furs or conquest, but to save the souls of those whom they called "the Savages."*

To succeed, they had to learn the "Savages' " often scatological tongues and study their religious and tribal customs. These letters, the only real record of the early Indians of North America, introduce us to a people who

---

* In the early part of the seventeenth century the native people of Canada were not known to the French as "Indians," but by the names of their tribal confederacies, and were referred to collectively as "Les Sauvages" (the Savages). The natives, for their part, spoke of the French as "Normans" and of the Jesuit fathers as "Blackrobes." As for the obscene language used by the natives at that time, it was a form of rough banter and was not intended to give offense. I am aware that I have taken a novelist's license in the question of Algonkian understanding of Iroquoian speech.

bear little relationship to the "Red Indians" of fiction and folklore. The Huron, Iroquois, and Algonkin were a handsome, brave, incredibly cruel people who, at that early stage, were in no way dependent on the white man and, in fact, judged him to be their physical and mental inferior. They were warlike; they practiced ritual cannibalism and, for reasons of religion, subjected their enemies to prolonged and unbearable tortures. Yet, as parents, they could not bear to strike or reprove their unruly children. They were pleasure-loving and polygamous, sharing sexual favors with strangers as freely as they shared their food and hearth. They despised the "Blackrobes" for their habit of hoarding possessions. They also held the white man in contempt for his stupidity in not realizing that the land, the rivers, the animals, were all possessed of a living spirit and subject to laws that must be respected.

From the works of anthropologists and historians who have established many facts about Indian behavior not known to the early Jesuits, I was made doubly aware of the strange and gripping tragedy that occurred when the Indian belief in a world of night and in the power of dreams clashed with the Jesuits' preachments of Christianity and a paradise after death. This novel is an attempt to show that each of these beliefs inspired in the other fear, hostility, and despair, which later would result in the destruction and abandonment of the Jesuit missions, and the conquest of the Huron people by the Iroquois, their deadly enemy.

▼

While much of the information contained in this novel on the mores, beliefs, and language of both "Savages" and Jesuits comes from the *Relations*, I am also indebted to other sources. I would like to thank James Hunter, Research Curator of Sainte Marie Among the Hurons, and also Bill Byrick, Professor Bruce Trigger of McGill University, and Professor W. J. Eccles of the College of William and Mary for assistance on various points.

I am indebted to Le Conseil des Arts du Canada for making it possible for me to visit places in Canada where records are kept of Iroquois, Algonkin, and Huron history and customs, and the sites of early Iroquois and Huron settlements, in particular, the village of Midland, Ontario, where the Ontario government has accurately reconstructed longhouses, a village, and the original Jesuit mission established there.

ONE

Laforgue felt his body tremble. What can be keeping them? Has the Commandant refused? Why has he not sent for me? Is this God's punishment for my lie about my hearing? But it wasn't a lie; my intention was honorable. Or is that a sophistry? Am I now so mired in my ambition that I can no longer tell truth from falsehood?

For what seemed the hundredth time, the sentry on duty outside the Commandant's quarters turned and marched along the ramparts of the fort. Laforgue heard voices. He looked down the steep path which led to the wooden buildings of the settlement. Two men were coming up. One was an officer, his slouch hat tilted over his forehead, his uniform whitened by dust. When Laforgue saw the face of the second man, he felt a sudden disquiet. A month ago, this man, a fur trader named Massé, had run from the stinking wineshop where the traders drank to yell obscene insults at Laforgue. The insults concerned a Savage girl Massé had been sleeping with, a girl Laforgue had lately tried to instruct in the faith.

Now, seeking to avoid further taunts, he moved closer to the shadow of the ramparts. And as he did, he looked up at the Commandant's quarters. Framed in a window was the face of Champlain.

▼

The Commandant, sitting at his window, saw a wide-brimmed clerical hat tilt up to reveal the pale, bearded visage of Father Laforgue. He looked past the lonely figure of the priest to the settlement of Québec, a jumble of wooden buildings, three hundred feet below. As in a painting, his eye was led toward the curve of the great river where four French ships lay at anchor. In a week they would be gone.

Behind him, he heard the Jesuit Superior cough, a small reminder, deferential yet impatient. "You were saying, Commandant?"

"I said it is late in the year. Tell them that."

The Jesuit, Father Bourque, translated for the Savages. Chomina, the elder Savage, had shaved his head bald except for a ridge of hair, which bristled across the crown like the spine of a hedgehog. His face was a mask of white clay. The younger, a leader called Neehatin, had ornamented himself for this occasion by drawing rings of yellow ochre around his eyes and painting his nose a bright blue. Both watched Champlain as they might a large and unpredictable animal. When the Jesuit had finished, the younger Savage spoke. Champlain turned to him as a deaf man toward moving lips. In all these years, he, the founder of this land, had not mastered the Savage tongue.

"He asks if Agnonha no longer wishes them to carry the French," Father Bourque said.

"Why would he ask that?"

"I think they are worried that you will not give them the six muskets they have requested," the Jesuit said. "As you know, your Excellency, this is the real reason they have offered to help us."

Champlain smiled at the Savage. "Tell him Agnonha is grateful for his offer of help. Tell him that for once Agnonha may be willing to offer muskets as presents. But tell him my concern is this. To succeed, the journey should have started three weeks ago."

"With respect," Father Bourque said, "I think there is still time to reach the Ihonatiria mission. As you know, I have twice made this journey myself."

Champlain looked at the priest's black cassock and thought, irreverently, that it reminded him of a schoolboy's smock. When you were still a boy in school, Father, I made and mapped the journey of which you speak. What do you know of that time? Why do you think these Savages want muskets? It is not to hunt but to kill their enemies.

"It is not just the onset of winter," he told the Jesuit. "There is the other, the greater danger. We have not spoken of that."

The Jesuit bowed his head. "The journey, like our lives, is in God's hands."

"But what if there is no mission? What if Laforgue arrives to find the two Fathers dead?"

"We will cross that bridge when we come to it."

Champlain fingered his graying beard in a gesture which semaphored his irritation. "Not *we*," he said. "It is Father Laforgue who must cross it. I do not know him well, but certainly he has no experience of these hardships."

"Would you wish to question him, your Excellency? I have brought him with me. He waits outside."

"What can I learn from that? I have said he has no experience of the great river."

"In my opinion," the Jesuit said, "he is adequate to the task. He is an ordained member of the Society of Jesus and, as such, his capabilities have been carefully assessed by the Order."

"You are talking of assessments which were made in France. I am talking of dangers and sufferings the Society of Jesus has not dreamed of."

"With respect," Father Bourque said. "There are few hardships not envisaged or experienced by our members in different lands."

Champlain looked at the Savages, who squatted on the floor, their knees as high as their heads. The Savages considered it ill-mannered to parley while standing. While he had been careful to remain seated, the Jesuit carelessly paced the room. "The young man you are sending with him is a boy, not yet twenty," Champlain said.

"True. But he is an exceptional young man."

"In what way is he exceptional, Father?"

"He was sent out as a workman, but with the highest recommendations. He is devout and diligent. His uncle, a priest, instructed him in Latin, and he studied with the Récollet Fathers in Rouen."

"Latin will not help him on the great river."

"No. But he is highly intelligent and adaptable. When I discovered his talent for languages, I sent him off to spend time with the Algonkin at their eel fishery. In a year he has mastered Algonkian and Huron speech."

Champlain heard a sudden noise. It was the noise of a wooden bowl striking against the floor. The Savages had begun to gamble, shaking the bowl and examining the plum stones in it. The stones were painted white on one side, black on the other. The gamble was to guess which color predominated. "Father," he said. "We have talked too long in our tongue. They are weary of us."

"True. My apologies."

Again, the bowl banged on the floor. Champlain felt a familiar numbness move up his arm. Will this be my last winter? Will I never again see the red flame of Richelieu's robe come toward me in the long gallery of the Palais de Justice, passing all those who seek his ear? I bend to kiss his ring; he smiles at me, a smile that tells nothing of the smiler's thought. Who will he send here to replace me? And what would he say to this request? The journey to almost certain death of a priest and a boy, against the chance to save a small outpost for France and for the Faith. In the conquest of a nation, lives are currency.

He had his answer. He smiled at the painted faces. "Tell them six muskets. No more."

Laforgue, watching, at last saw the Superior and the Savages emerge from the Commandant's quarters.

Is it yes or no? Why did he not send for me? Quickly, he walked along beneath the ramparts, controlling his desire to break into a run. The Superior, passing the guard, turned to the Savages, but the Savages, whose custom it was not to utter formal farewells, simply walked away. They did not use the path which led down to the settlement, but went across the rougher terrain which led to their encampment.

Father Bourque looked back when he heard Laforgue's footstep. "Ah, there you are," he said. "Come. We must hurry."

He moved past Laforgue, going down the path. Laforgue, trained in the rule of obedience, did not ask the question which consumed his thoughts, but fell in a pace behind him. They passed by the officer and Massé, who, coming up, bowed respectfully to the Superior. Massé did not look at Laforgue. In silence, the two priests continued down to the jetty, where their canoe was moored. Father Bourque waited while Laforgue untied the rope and, draping his wooden clogs around his neck so as not to damage the thin bark bottom, stepped neatly into the birch-bark craft, and held it steady against the mooring place. Father Bourque, also removing his clogs, got into the front of the canoe as Laforgue, kneeling precisely as the Savages had taught him, carefully moved the craft out onto the river. He heeled it toward a tributary which led downstream to the Jesuit residence. Father Bourque took up his paddle. Steadily they stroked toward the far bank of the tributary, where a rectangle of wooden palisades enclosed two buildings which formed the residence. Laforgue, aware that the Superior was judging his skills, rose up at the precise moment the swift canoe glided to shore and leaped onto the landing place, neatly catching the prow and guiding it in.

"Where is Daniel?" Father Bourque asked, as he disembarked.

"I believe they are all working up at the storehouse."

"All of them?" The Superior did not wait for a reply but set off along the narrow track which led to the residence. As they entered the long-grassed meadows surrounding the palisades, a miasma of mosquitoes clouded about them, causing them to slap their faces, duck and proceed, half running, toward the gate. "Find Daniel and bring him to me," the Superior said.

Inside the gate they separated, Father Bourque entering the principal building, a one-story construction of wooden planks, plastered with mud and thatched with grasses. Laforgue hurried on to the second building, half burned some years back by the English, a building the Jesuits' workmen were now repairing. As he approached, he heard the sound of hammering and laughter; someone shouted something in the Breton tongue. Escaping the mosquito cloud, he ducked under the hanging which served for a door. As he did, the laughter and hammering ceased and from their perches and workbenches the men looked down at him in silence.

"What news, Father?"

The head carpenter had asked the question, but Laforgue looked at Daniel Davost, who stood, holding a plank, his mouth full of nails.

"No news yet," Laforgue said. "But Father Bourque wants to see Daniel at once."

"Then you're going," the carpenter said. The other workmen exchanged glances. All of them disapproved of the priests' sending a young boy on this dangerous journey. And now, as Daniel left with Laforgue, angry voices were raised, speaking Breton, which Laforgue did not understand.

"What did they say, Daniel?"

"Nothing, Father. Some joke."

Outside, in the choking swarm of insects, they ran toward the main residence. As they entered they passed through the chapel, a small bare room with a wooden altar on which were two cloth hangings; one represented the Holy Spirit in the form of a dove, the other an image of the Virgin. The chapel opened into the refectory, which the priests used also as their workroom. In this room twelve Savage men and women squatted on the ground in a semicircle, just inside the doorway. They did not move when Daniel and Laforgue entered but kept their eyes on a clock which sat on the refectory table. The smell of their unwashed bodies and greasy hair filled the room with a pungent sickly odor. Two other priests, Fathers Bonnet and Meynard, were in the adjoining kitchen together with a lay brother.

"I have brought Daniel, Father," Laforgue said.

The Superior, who was working at the refectory table, turned and pointed to the clock. The hands stood at two minutes to four. Laforgue nodded to show he understood. All waited in silence, watching the clock.

These Savages, unlike those who had attended on

the Commandant, wore no paint. They were in their normal summer garb, the men naked except for a breech clout, the women covered modestly enough in long tunics made of animal skins. All were filthy, their hair matted with food particles, their skin greased to keep off flies and mosquitoes. And yet, despite this, their slender bodies, their lack of facial hair, and an absence of physical deformities made them seem more handsome and of a higher species than the priests of the residence.

Now, as the hands of the clock moved toward four, one of the male Savages rose and walked around it, then went into the chapel to see if anyone was hiding there. Satisfied, he returned, nodding to the others. In the kitchen, the priests ceased their labors and fell silent. All waited in a quiet in which the only sound was the ticking of the clock.

The clock chimed: *Dong! Dong! Dong! Dong!* At the stroke of four, the Superior cried out, "Stop!"

The chime died. The clock's steady ticking was heard. The Savages gave a cry of astonishment and delight, turning to each other with the amazement of people who have witnessed a miracle. The eldest male Savage began to speak to the others. "You see, it's just as I fucking well told you. The Captain is alive. The Captain spoke. I told you. He spoke."

The Savages smiled and exchanged glances of pleasure. An old woman laughed. "Shit," she said. "What did he say?"

All turned to the Superior, who now raised his head from the writing of his letter. In the Savage tongue, Father Bourque replied, "He says it is time to go. He says, 'Get up and go home.'"

At once, chattering among themselves, the deputation of Savages rose. They approached the clock shyly, peering at it, not daring to touch it. Then, obedient to its command, they filed out of the refectory, going through the chapel to the front door, which Father Bonnet held open as he bade them farewell.

Daniel Davost heard the slap of the bolt in the lock as Father Bonnet shut the door: a jailer sound. He saw the priests come from their tasks to gather in the refectory. *Now it will be told.* He shivered, as though the locked door had shut him into a prison from which there was no escape. *What will I do if the journey is canceled? The Algonkin will gather by the river and slip away at dawn. She will be among them; she kneels in Chomina's canoe, head bent, plying a paddle. She will not look back. There are no farewells in their lives. Last night in our stifling room, twelve snoring workmen above and around me, I spat in Jesus' face, I who once was pure, who now desire to go on this journey not for God's glory but for the most base and sinful reason.*

He turned to look at the Superior, who still penned his letter. His alarm turned to panic. *What if the journey is canceled? I will run away.*

▼

Father Bourque wrote on, his quill pen covering page after page in haste, for this report must be made as full as possible. That was what the Order wished. In the past few days he had labored on it in every spare moment, for it must leave with the ships next week. This report Father Provincial in France would distribute widely among the faithful and powerful as an inspiration for funds and volunteers to aid in the work of saving souls. In his neat hand, Father Bourque set down the subject of his greatest concern.

Two weeks ago there came here from the country of the Hurons a Savage, baptized in the faith by Father Brabant. This Savage, by name Ihongwaha, brought to us a letter from Father Brabant, who ministers to the Savages in the region of Ossossané. It is a request that we send as soon as possible a replacement for Father Jerome, who is ill in the northern part of that country in a place called Ihonatiria. Father Brabant also writes that there is a sickness or fever now general in the whole region and that the sorcerers of the Huron people have accused the "Blackrobes" (our Fathers) of bringing this illness. Father Brabant writes that a Savage of the Ihonatiria region, baptized a Christian, arrived at Ossossané with news that the chiefs, after a council, sent word to Father Jerome that if their young warriors decided to put a hatchet in his head and in the head of Father Duval, his assistant, they would have nothing to say about it. Father Brabant writes that, plagued as his own region is with this fever, he will not find it possible to visit the northern region to ascertain the Fathers' fate. He asks that we send at once a priest to carry on the mission at Ihonatiria in the event that the illness of Father Jerome has proved fatal, or in the event that he and Father Duval have been martyred. We have been much disturbed by this news and have asked the help of the Sieur de Champlain in persuading a

*party of Algonkian hunters to take one of our Fa-
thers with them on the annual journey to their winter hunting grounds, and, further, to provide
paddlers to take the Father on to the top of the
Great Rapids, whence the Allumette people will
help him proceed. And so, with the good offices of
the Sieur de Champlain we have decided—*

"Father Bourque?"

The Superior looked up. He saw that the refectory
was now filled with the priests of the mission and that
the youth, Daniel Davost, was also present. The Superior shook some sand on his writings, then stood and,
turning to the company, made the sign of the cross. "Let
us pray," he said, and began, in Latin. When the prayer
was finished, he again made the sign of the cross. "We
have given thanks because it has pleased God to grant
our request."

At once, the room filled with excited murmurings.
"Yes," said Father Bourque. "The Commandant has
agreed to the Savages' requests for presents, including
six muskets and some powder and shot. He will also give
the customary departure feast. Father Bonnet?"

"Yes, Father?"

"We will make some contribution to this feast. You
will discuss it with the cook of the garrison. Now, sit
down, everyone."

Obediently the company took their places around
the refectory table. "We must decide now what must be
got ready and what can be carried in the canoes," the Superior said. "As, at best, you will travel with only two
canoes from the point at which the Algonkin leave you

at the head of the rapids, we must choose carefully. You will take clothing for the mission and, in addition, a chalice, a monstrance, four missals, two sets of mass vestments, writing materials, and two gallons of altar wine. You will also take trading goods: tobacco, awls, beads, knives, hatchets. As for food, we will prepare enough corn meal for their sagamité gruel to feed the entire party for the twenty days it will take to reach the top of the rapids. You will take a change of clothing and cloaks for the winter ahead. All these things, with the exception of the food, must not be more than can be placed in one canoe in the event that the Savages desert you. At the worst, you must be able to paddle and portage one canoe and its contents."

"What about snowshoes, Father?" Laforgue asked.

There was laughter. Everyone had watched Laforgue practice daily in the long grasses of the meadows, his feet attached to the strange thong and wooden *raquettes* with which the Savages traveled the winter snows, lifting his legs like some strange seabird in a marsh.

"Yes, take them," Father Bourque said. "Oh, and Daniel? When we are finished here I want to see you for a moment."

The talk went on, but Daniel no longer heard what was said. *I want to see you for a moment.* Someone, one of the Algonkin up at the fishery, must have said something in a joke to one of the fur traders, who may have told one of the priests, who would at once be in duty bound to tell the Superior, who now will confront me. And he will know that I have lied, and I have not confessed, that I have sinned and sinned and cannot stop.

Which of the priests was responsible? Father Laforgue? No, he would have shown it in his manner as we came here today.

And now, ending the discussion, the Superior beckoned Daniel to follow him. In panic, his mouth dry, he rose and followed Father Bourque out of the residence, going toward a small storage shed where the priests sometimes heard confessions. The choice of this shed as a place to parley could only mean that he had been discovered. They entered. The Superior shut the door. He gestured to Daniel to take the solitary stool, sat himself down on an upended plow, shipped from France eight years ago but not yet used in this inhospitable climate, and hitched up his cassock, revealing bare ankles, cruelly swollen by mosquito bites.

"Tell me, Daniel, why do you want to make this journey?"

The question hung in the air. Daniel forced himself to look at the Superior. *Someone has told him. He must know.* "Why do you ask, Father?" He heard his voice waver as he spoke.

"Because I must decide. When I spoke today with the Sieur de Champlain, he warned me of the great dangers and mentioned your youth. It is true that you are very young."

"I do not feel young," Daniel said. Relief made him want to burst out laughing. *He knows nothing. He knows nothing, after all!*

But it was Father Bourque who laughed, throwing back his head and showing carious teeth. "That proves you are still a boy. But you haven't answered my question. *Why* do you want to make this journey?"

Daniel hesitated, then said, as a child says its catechism. "For the greater glory of God."

I spit on Jesus' face as I tell that lie.

"But you are not a Jesuit."

"I wish to serve God. That is why I asked to be sent to New France."

"Yes. Of course. Of course." The Superior bent down and scratched his bitten ankles. "Well then, I will make you a promise. If, at the end of a year, you still have this wish, we will do what we can to help you. We will bring you back from Ihonatiria and send you to France to study for the priesthood. Would that please you, Daniel?"

"Yes, Father." He knows nothing. He sees me black-robed, devout, his younger self, prostrate before the altar as I take my priestly vows. As last year I saw myself, when I knelt in the Church of the Blessed Virgin in Honfleur, my arms outstretched in adoration of my Savior, making my vow to spend two years serving God in a distant land.

"Are your parents alive?" Father Bourque asked.

"No, Father. My nearest relative is my uncle, the priest I told you about."

"The one who taught you Latin. So if anything happens to you, which God forbid, he is the one I must write to?"

"Yes, Father."

"God bless you, then," the Superior said. "Oh, and Daniel? Send Father Laforgue to me. I will wait for him here."

▼

Savage drumbeats punctuated drunken Breton songs. Mosquitoes and tiny midges moved in separate clouds as they sought out blood. The day had been warm but an evening coolness came in from the river, bringing relief to the Commandant and the Savage leaders, who sat in a circle on the riverbank; Champlain upright in an armchair, wearing a cloak made of beaver skins. Outside this circle, the Jesuits of the mission huddled as though beleaguered, drab figures in long black cassocks, their wide-brimmed hats looped up at the sides. Farther down the riverbank, the majority of the population of New France, some one hundred colonists, artisans, fur company employees and soldiers, strolled about among the remaining Savages of the Algonkian band, who were now eating their share of the Commandant's feast. These, the younger men, together with the women and children, crowded around a bank of smoking fires on which were placed cooking kettles containing a stinking mess of bear meat, fat, fish, and sagamité. The Savages ate gluttonously from the kettles, stopping from time to time to wipe their greasy fingers on their hair or on the coats of their dogs, which ran barking around the fires in search of discarded scraps.

In the center of the council circle, Samuel de Champlain looked to his interpreter, who gave a slight nod, warning that the time had come for him to speak. He rose, bowed to the leaders, then settled himself again in his armchair and beckoned to the group of priests. At once, Father Paul Laforgue rose and came to the Commandant's side, a slight, pale man, thin-bearded, intellectual, but with a strange determination in the eyes and narrow mouth. Champlain turned to the Savage leaders and pointed to Father Bourque and the other Jesuits. "These are our Fathers," Champlain said. "We love them more than we love ourselves. The whole of the French nation loves them. They do not go among you for your furs. They have left their friends and their country to show you the way to heaven. If you love the French as you say you love them, then love and honor these, our Fathers. And, in particular, I, Agnonha, commend to you Father Laforgue, who is going far into the land of the Hurons. I say to those of you who will accompany him on his journey, guard him well. And now I place this beloved Father in your care."

As the speech was translated, sentence by sentence, the assembly of Savages uttered the cutomary ejaculations of approval. The guttural sounds reminded Champlain of animals groaning in pain, but he smiled contentedly. They also meant the journey had been approved.

Two leaders rose and squatted before him. One began to speak. In the traditional manner of the Savages, he first repeated what Champlain had said and then summarized what had been said on this subject on previous occasions. The Savages, having no written language, conducted all their affairs in this manner, constantly astonishing the French by their remarkable feats of recall. The leader went on to proclaim Algonkian fealty to the French in general and to Champlain in particular. His speech recalled the time, more than twenty-five years before, when Champlain, whom the Savages called Agnonha, or "Iron Man," had buckled on his steel armor and gone forth with the Algonkin and Huron to fight against and kill the Iroquois, their traditional enemy.

When the speech was finished, Champlain uttered some words of gratitude, then rose to signal an end to the parley. At once, Chomina and Neehatin, the leaders of the hunting party that would accompany Laforgue, went to the priest and embraced him as a sign that he had been given into their trust.

Satisfied, Champlain signaled to his officers and left the gathering. As he walked under the balcony of the trading post of the Company of One Hundred Associates of New France, Martin Doumergue, the chief clerk of the post, rose and bowed to his Excellency. Behind Doumergue, Pierre Tallevant, his assistant, newly arrived from France, concealed a half-filled bottle of brandy behind his back as he bowed in turn. Both men watched as the Commandant and his officers set off up the steep path in the direction of Champlain's fort.

"Why is the Commandant dressed like a Savage?" Tallevant asked, as he again produced the bottle and filled his superior's glass.

Doumergue laughed. "You mean the fur robe? It's a present from the chiefs. Anyway, it's symbolic, isn't it?"

"What do you mean?"

"I mean, without the fur trade none of us would be in this colony."

"Colony?" Tallevant said. "Why do they call it a colony? Look at that mob out there. Where are the colonists? Where are the families who're going to settle this place? The English have colonists, the Dutch have colonists, but what do we have? Fur traders and priests."

Doumergue drank, then placed his glass on the railing of the balcony. "Do you blame us?" he asked. "I mean, would you bring a woman out here? I want to show you something."

Unsteady in drink, Tallevant rose and went to the railing.

"Look over there," Doumergue said. "See that Savage with a musket on his back?"

"The one eating from the kettle?"

"Right. Know who that is? It's Jean Mercier."

"What are you talking about?"

"That's Mercier, I tell you," Doumergue said. "He's just been up-country with one of their hunting parties, buying pelts. See? He dresses like them now. He even eats their food."

Tallevant stared uneasily at the almost naked figure biting into a piece of bear meat, the animal hair still on the half-cooked flesh. The man wore European hunting boots, not the soft shoes made of skins which a real Savage would use. Could this be the Rouennais fur trader whose accounts Tallevant had seen entered in the Company's ledgers in Caen? He turned to Doumergue. "What happened to him? Is he drunk or mad?"

"No, no. He likes the life."

"But how can he? That stinking food, the flies, the smells, the way they live."

"The way they live?" Martin Doumergue laughed. "They live for their pleasure, for a full belly. They live to hunt and fish. They do no work, the Algonkin. And, most important, they let him fuck their young girls. He likes that. He likes to hunt, he likes to get away from the life the priests would have us live here, praying and fasting and all that. He's free up there. And he's not the only one. I have twenty-one traders on my books. In five years, if they stay here, most of them will be like Mercier."

"I don't believe it," Tallevant said.

"And if we do bring in colonists," Doumergue said, "the same thing will happen to them. Do you think I'd bring a woman out and marry her and settle here? What for? So that my sons will grow up half savage, running naked in the woods, then dying of starvation when the snows come?"

Uneasily, Tallevant looked back at the tall figure of the trader, the lank greasy hair, the thin loins, the buttocks bare beneath the breechclout. Doumergue is wrong; it must be drink or madness. To go from all that we know and are back to that brutish state? "It makes no sense," he said aloud.

"Doesn't it? It makes sense to me. We're not colonizing the Savages. They're colonizing us. Even the Commandant in that smelly fur robe is happier here than he ever was in France."

Tallevant refilled his glass and drank. The brandy fumes rose in his head. "Well, not me," he said. "When my contract is up, I'm going home."

Martin Doumergue looked at him. "Will you? I wonder. Will any of us?"

▼

The two Savages who had risen to embrace Paul Laforgue at the conclusion of the Commandant's feast now led him to the temporary encampment of the Algonkin, their brightly painted faces grinning in a manner which made him think of medieval masquers on feast days in his native Normandy. As he entered the encampment he was surrounded by a crowd of Savage women, the married ones prematurely aged and worn by toil, the young girls shamefully loose in their clothing, brazen and care-free as the gleeful, unruly Savage children who ran be-hind him, pinching and pulling him as though he were a toy for their amusement. Straining to hear through the dull ringing of his infected left ear, Laforgue understood that the Savage women were asking what food he would bring on the journey, would he have tobacco, did he have brandy to give them. Faces crowded close, white teeth set off by sun-browned skin, handsome, merry dark eyes, long dark hair: these faces, these people will be my only companions, save Daniel, when tomorrow we set out upriver.

Laforgue had never lived in an encampment of Sav-ages. With the exception of Father Bourque, none of the priests now in the Québec residence had traveled as he would travel, sleeping outdoors or in Savage shelters, eating only Savage food. "It is travel of the most difficult sort," the Superior had warned him. "Yet it is also the most advantageous way in which to make the journey. For if you travel with a hunting party of men, women and children, there is always the chance that, if a child or an adult fall ill en route, a soul can be gained for God by a deathbed baptism. Father Brabant and others have written in the *Relations* that each time they journeyed to the Huron lands they had the great privilege of saving at least one soul in this manner. Remember, such a blessing will more than justify all the perils and discomforts you may suffer."

Now, remembering the Superior's words, Laforgue forced a smile as he endured the badgering of the Savage children: one tugging at the beads of his rosary as if to break them; another pulling at his beard and calling him a hairy dog, for the Savages were not bearded and pulled out their own sparse facial hair, considering it to be ugly. A third child, a giggling little girl, kept trying to slip her hand through the buttons of Laforgue's cassock and fondle his genitals. The Savages paid no attention to this, for it was unheard of for them to punish or restrain their children in any way. And so, as the little imp persisted, Laforgue lifted her up and put her aside, then tried to make his way clear of the crowd. But the Savage women laughingly restrained him and now, thinking longingly of his cell, where at this hour he would kneel alone in a time of prayer, he decided to invoke Captain Clock. Raising his hands as if to address the crowd, he shouted, "Wait! Captain Clock says I must go home. Captain says it is time for me to go."

"Where is the Captain?" an old Savage woman asked. "Are you hiding the Captain now?"

"No, the Captain is in our house. But he spoke this morning. Excuse me, I must go now."

"*Dong! Dong! Dong! Dong!*" The old woman, her face a web of tiny creases, imitated the sound of the striking clock in a manner inhuman in its accuracy.

"Stop!" cried a Savage after the fourth sound. All exploded in laughter. Chomina, the leader who had escorted Laforgue into the encampment, took him by the hand and cleared a passage for him among the laughing throng. "Go then, Nicanis," he said, using the name the Algonkin had given Laforgue. "Go home to the Captain and tell him that tomorrow, at first light, we await you here."

"Till tomorrow," Laforgue said. The Savages were still. Even the children ceased their movements. They stood, watching him in silence, as he walked away from their fires, going downriver to the place where the traders lay about drinking. As Laforgue approached this place, he saw Daniel, standing in the shadow of the trees, waiting for him.

"I have a canoe, Father. I will take you back to the residence."

"Good," Laforgue said, then looked at the boy. "Is something wrong?"

"No, Father."

But something *was* wrong, he was sure of it. It was as though Daniel were fearful, and as they continued on he saw that the boy moved high on the riverbank as though to avoid the place between the trees where the traders were. A sensible precaution, no doubt, for one could never be sure of the traders' mood, especially when it was a public holiday and they had been drinking. As though to confirm this thought, male voices shouted and then Laforgue heard a sudden scream. A Savage girl ran out from the trees, long-legged and awkward as a foal about to fall. The girl was tall and slender and dressed for some Savage ceremony, wearing only a short kilt from waist to knee and a collar and necklace of the blue and purple beads which the Savages fashioned from the inside of shells. She ran directly toward Laforgue and Daniel, then swerved as though they were a wall, twisting about to run away downriver. As she did, Laforgue saw a Savage come from the trees in pursuit. The Savage was drunk; he wore hunting boots which were not made for running and now, as he lurched past Laforgue, he skidded and fell, his half-naked body subsiding in a dusty cloud near the soft mud of the river's edge. Laforgue looked at Daniel, who, ignoring the fallen Savage, was staring after the fleeing girl. He took the boy's arm, seeking to hurry him away from these occasions of lust, but as they passed the sprawled figure of the Savage, the man twisted around and caught the skirt of Laforgue's cassock, forcing him to stop. The Savage looked up, his eyes muddied with drink, then said in French, "Bless me, Father, for I have sinned."

"Come, Father," Daniel said. "Pay no attention."

"Wait." Laforgue stared in astonishment at the Savage. "You speak French?"

"Imperfectly," said the Savage. "And I would prefer not to."

At once, Laforgue knelt beside the man and made the sign of the cross, for this Savage must be a Christian. Where did he come from, how did he learn such good French, how did he know, in French, those words which were a request that a priest hear one's confession? "I cannot confess you now, my son," Laforgue said gently. "You are drunk."

The Savage smiled. Suddenly, behind him in the trees, Laforgue heard laughter and knew that he had been played a trick. This Savage was not an Algonkin but one of those renegade French traders, the coureurs de bois, who went in the woods with the Savages and affected their heathen ways. And as Laforgue turned to see who mocked him, half a dozen other men of this sort came from the trees. With them were three half-naked Savage girls. The traders were half-stripped themselves, their hair and bodies decked with Savage feathers and colored beads. All were drunk.

It was no place for a priest. "Come, Daniel," he said,

but as he tried to rise from his kneeling position, the false Savage pulled again on his cassock, causing him to stumble before he managed to free himself.

Daniel had already gone ahead, and as Laforgue started after him, the traders' laughter loud in his ears, he saw the boy run in the direction of the Savage girl, who had circled and was coming back. Daniel began calling out to her, and so Laforgue turned his good ear in that direction. But heard, as so often in the past weeks, only a dull, distant sound. What was Daniel saying? He should not speak to her. She might be drunk. In drink, the Savages believed that a devil took possession of them. If a drunken Savage killed another, the Savages did not hold him responsible for his action, and so it was dangerous to go near them when they were in that condition. But as Laforgue drew closer he saw Daniel grip the girl's arm.

"Let her be," he called.

"Go back to your people," Daniel said, and this time Laforgue heard his words. "Go on, go at once." He looked as though he would strike the girl, but at that moment she twisted free of his grip and ran to the renegade trader, who rose, lewdly holding out his arms in welcome, his breechclout awry, his penis erect and sticking up.

"Come away now," Laforgue said, his face hot with anger at the sight of the trader's shame. But Daniel moved ahead of him.

"Let me be," the boy said, but stared open-mouthed at the scene below them on the bank, the trader embracing the girl as she began to fondle his penis, he pulling her short skirt up over her buttocks.

It was a sight the devil had sent, and Laforgue would have none of it. With a strength that surprised him, he caught hold of Daniel and turned him away, saying, "Let's go back. We must get ready. We are leaving at first light tomorrow."

And saw in the boy's face a stupefaction as though the sight of lust had robbed him of all sense.

"Where is the canoe?" Laforgue asked. "Where did you leave the canoe?"

But the boy pulled back, as though to look again at the scene of lechery.

"Come away," Laforgue said. "Don't look at that. It is a sin to look."

"I *wasn't* looking," the boy said. There were tears in his eyes. "This way," he said, in an angry, strangled voice, and started off at a fast pace, leaving Laforgue behind as they ran to the place where the mission canoe was moored. Why was he crying? But then Laforgue reminded himself that Daniel was a sheltered child brought up by a priestly uncle in a small Norman village. What would a boy like that know of such lewd debauchery?

"You should punish him," the boy said suddenly, as he untied the canoe. "If you tell Father Bourque, Father Bourque will tell the Commandant and he will be put in the stocks. It's what he deserves. Disrespect for religion is a sin and forbidden."

"But Mercier is a Huguenot," Laforgue said. "He is not of our faith."

"Even so. It is forbidden. You should tell the Commandant."

"Yes, yes, it is my duty," Laforgue said. "But we

are leaving tomorrow and I have not time—I mean, I cannot find it in my heart. He was drunk. He was confused."

"Mercier confused?" Daniel said, pushing the canoe out into the shallows. He stood, steadying the canoe so that Laforgue could climb in. "Mercier doesn't give a damn, about God or France or anything. We should tell Father Bourque."

"Daniel," Laforgue said. "Father Bourque has enough to trouble him, don't you think?"

The boy, silent, bent over the prow of the canoe, paddling skillfully as a Savage.

"Tomorrow we start our journey," Laforgue said. "That is what we must think of now. Let us ask God's forgiveness for our sins and for this man's sins also. Don't you agree?"

At last, he saw Daniel half turn his head and nod agreement. But his body still shook with sobs. He is still a child, Laforgue reminded himself. It is my duty to protect him.

2

We are ready," Chomina said.

Neehatin did not answer. He was looking at the Blackrobes. The chief Blackrobe now stood near the water. The Blackrobe Nicanis and the Norman boy went down on their knees before him. The chief Blackrobe raised his right hand, the hand open like a knife. He made a downward movement, then a sideways movement. The two who knelt bowed their heads beneath this movement as the chief Blackrobe spoke some words in their tongue.

"What are they doing?" Chomina asked.

"It is some fucking sorcery," Neehatin told him.

"They make that sign to silence their enemies. You have divided their food up among our canoes?"

"I have done it."

"Where are the six muskets?"

"Three in my canoe, three in yours. And I have placed the powder and shot in a skin, as you said."

"We will not use the muskets until we reach the hunting ground," Neehatin said. "Those Norman pigs have given only half the powder and shot I asked for. Besides, we have to learn how to shoot them."

"The Norman boy knows how."

"Fuck him," Neehatin said. "We will learn ourselves."

He looked at the riverbank. The boy and the Blackrobe had risen from their knees, and now they went forward to put their arms around the chief Blackrobe as though he were some woman. Neehatin looked back at his own people. They waited. There were twenty-six, including women and children. He looked at the sky. The moon sat pale in the clouds as day came out of night. The sky gave no sign against their leaving.

Neehatin walked down to the Blackrobes. He smiled at them. "We are ready," he said.

▼

Laforgue knelt in the narrow canoe, the paddle resting on his knees, his wooden clogs tied around his neck, his head bare to the cool morning breeze. Behind him a Savage woman steadied the canoe with light strokes of her paddle. Three dogs sat on skins which covered the cargo, and at the front a male Savage held the craft in midstream, waiting, looking back to where the other canoes were moving off from shore. On the riverbank, Fathers Bourque, Bonnet and Meynard lined up in a row, waving their hats in a gesture of farewell. There were five canoes in all: the Savages traveled in family groups, the children and dogs sitting on the goods, the women paddling in the middle, the men in front and at the rear, steering and guiding the craft. Laforgue saw Daniel in the canoe behind his own and, ahead, Neehatin, the leader, who now raised his hand in a gesture which at once set all in movement. The canoes, incredibly light and fragile for their heavy burdens, glided swiftly into the slipstream, using the ebb flow to avoid moving against the main current. Laforgue looked back at the huddle of wooden settlements, at the steep cliffs and, above them, at the earth and timber ramparts enclosing the modest stone edifice of Champlain's fort, which was the principal building of New France. As he did, from the ramparts came a puff of smoke and the roar of cannon. Alarmed and astonished, the Savages looked up. Neehatin, standing in his canoe, called out that the cannon fire was an honor, a salute from the Normans for their journey. Delighted, laughing, the Savages bowed to their stroke. The canoes sped on. The Savages, as was their way, fell silent, the only noise now the slap of paddles in quiet waters.

Two years ago, before leaving France, Laforgue had journeyed to his home in Rouen to say an anniversary mass for the repose of his dead father's soul. After the ceremony, he and his mother walked back to her house, passing through the Place du Vieux Marché. It was a wet and windy spring day; rain beat on the roofs of the timbered Norman houses in the square. His mother, holding her cloak over her head, turned from her normal homeward path and crossed the square to that spot, marked by a cross, where, two hundred years before, faggots had been piled high to burn Saint Joan of Arc at the stake. His mother stopped at this holy place and, in the driving rain, knelt in prayer while Laforgue stood, awkward, not wanting to interrupt her devotions, not willing to kneel on the wet cobbles amid passing strangers. When she rose, her skirts wet, her stockings awry, his mother turned to him and said, "I prayed for you, Paul. I prayed for you here. Do you know why?"

"No, *maman.*"

"Because God has chosen you, just as He chose the Maid."

Her words made him blush. Surely it was foolish to compare him with a saint like Joan of Arc, but still it was true that ever since the Order had granted his petition to be sent to New France he had dreamed of the glory of martyrdom in that faraway land.

"Come," he said, taking her arm. "Let's go home. You're soaking. You will get your death of cold."

His mother gripped him tightly as they set off. "Promise me," she said. "Promise that when you go there, you will remember me in your daily prayers."

"Of course, of course," he said. "I always do, *maman.*"

"No, no, listen to me. God will hear your prayer as He will not hear mine. He will hear you as He did the Maid. For He has chosen you to die for Him. I will never see you again."

"*Maman,* please. You mustn't compare me with Saint Joan. I'm not a saint. Come. Let's go home."

Now in the silence of the great river, watching a flock of geese fly over distant treetops, Laforgue heard again his mother's words. In the past two years, living in the residence at Québec, every waking moment had been a preparation for this day: the time spent learning the unwritten Algonkian and Huron tongues, studying the writings of Father Brabant on the customs and language of the Savage peoples, the hours of practice in canoes, a scrupulous diligence in all tasks assigned to him, no matter how onerous or menial, and, above all, constant daily prayer, beseeching Saint Joseph and the Virgin to intercede on his behalf and grant him the honor of some greater danger in a lonely place. From the day the Savage, Ihongwaha, brought Father Brabant's letter telling of sickness in the Huron country, he had prayed in nightly vigils that he would be the chosen one. For, indeed, this was a journey like those he had read of long ago in the Jesuit house in Dieppe, a mission worthy of the Order's heroic martyrs in Paraguay, a mission to the very place where Father Brabant labored, he whom the Hurons revered, whose letters published in the *Relations* were an inspiration to all at home in France. And now his prayers had been answered. Today he set out for that place where martyrdom was more than just a pious hope. This is my hour. This is my beginning.

The day passed. The sun, high in the sky, dipped until it barely cleared the tops of the trees. A wind rippled the water into waves, a wind which numbed Laforgue's cheeks. He remembered what Father Bourque had told him of a second false summer which came in mid-October, bringing a few days of heat at the end of the autumnal season. That false summer was ending. Winter was near.

The sun fell below the tree line. Shadows moved across the surface of the water. Neehatin called out a command and at once the canoes turned, gliding toward a small tributary inlet. There, the Savages disembarked, pulling their canoes clear of the water. Laforgue, his limbs aching from hours of kneeling, walked stiffly up to the clearing where the Algonkin, with the ordered bustle of long practice, had begun to make preparations for camp. Neehatin and Chomina, the captains, assembled the men and then dispersed them among the trees. Some carried bows and arrows, others long spears like javelins, others hatchets and clubs. Daniel, taking his gun, joined one of the groups but called to Laforgue, "Stay here, Father. They say there is a chance of game. We'll be back in an hour or so."

"Will I come with you?"

The boy shook his head. Men and dogs disappeared in the undergrowth. A sudden clamor of voices filled the clearing as women passed by, carrying long poles of spruce saplings which they had just cut down. Laforgue sat for a moment watching the noisy children run about in the open space; then, remembering that it would soon be dark, he began to read his breviary. But the familiar book seemed strange in this place, and the Latin sentences jumbled in his head.

He looked up. In the center of the clearing some of the younger women had raised the long poles to converge in a sort of roof, while older ones brought from the canoes sheets of birch bark, which they unrolled, and then assembled to make the walls of the habitation. Still others dragged green spruce boughs from the nearby forest, spreading them in a vast carpet to provide a bed on which all could sleep. The work was long and arduous. The horizon took on the pale pink blush of the dying sun.

He looked at the words on his page and thought of the Jesuit house in Dieppe at this the hour of the evening office, when priests walked in the cloister, reading their breviaries, silent and absorbed. He had been one of them. But from now on he would read his office in some clearing in a strange forest, or behind the wooden palisades of a distant mission house. He looked again at the rabble of Savage women, emaciated, burdened by years of toil, limbs gnarled, faces worn by sun and wind; at the brown, laughing girls; at the children, wild as the forest which was their home. With these people he would live for years, perhaps for the rest of his life. A sudden sadness came upon him. He looked up at the pink orb of sky. A rush of tiny black birds whirled like commas across the clearing and disappeared among the treetops in a twittering swirl. He heard distant cries and, minutes later, the first male Savages came out of the forest. Their mood was jubilant. They held aloft, for the women's admiration, the slain bodies of hares and quail.

Fires were lit. The large kettles in which the Savages cooked all their food were brought up from the canoes and hung on poles which slanted over the fire. Gradually, as the sky darkened, the rest of the hunters returned. All were empty-handed until Chomina, the hunting captain, appeared with three other men, carrying on a long pole the slung body of a deer. Shouts of joy filled the air. The Algonkin butchered the deer and threw it into the kettles with the other carcasses. Then Laforgue saw Daniel come in empty-handed, stowing his gun in its hide pouch.

"Daniel?"

"Father Paul."

Daniel came over. He seemed distraught. He took off his beaver cap, and Laforgue noticed that he had braided his long hair in the Algonkian manner.

"They have killed a deer," Daniel said. "That means we will not make an early start tomorrow."

"But we must have an early start," Laforgue said. "I will speak to Neehatin. We must go at first light."

As he spoke, darkness seeped through the crepuscular light in the clearing. The bodies of the Savages became silhouettes, moving around the flame-lit circle of fires. Dogs ran about, barking, chased by children who tormented them. In the light of the fires, the faces of the older Savages seemed inhuman as wooden masks. Then, as the first pieces of half-cooked meat were taken from a pot, Neehatin rose, cut a slice from a haunch of deer, and came to Laforgue, holding it on his knife. "Here, Nicanis," he said. "Eat this. Now you will truly eat."

This was the Savage phrase of hospitality. Laforgue took the greasy meat in his hands. Hair and skin still adhered to it. "Now I will truly eat," he said and, conquering his nausea, bit into the half-cooked flesh. Men came up smiling, as Neehatin took a second piece of meat and gave it to Daniel, saying, "Now, Iwanchou," for this was the name the Algonkin had given the boy.

"Fucking good deer meat," one Savage said.

"Eat, fucking eat," another said.

Laforgue winced at the foul words. "They speak as dogs would speak, if they had tongues," Father Bourque had said about their filthy banter. "Remember it is not meant badly. We must ignore it. They will not change." He watched them eat. "Gluttony is their highest form of happiness," the Superior had told him. "They cannot be made to hoard their food against a time when there is none. Corn for their sagamité is the only food they will save." And Father Brabant, in his letters to Father Provincial, had once joked that the only prayer the Savages would make to God, was "Give us each day elk, beaver, and moose." Laforgue looked at the greasy half-cooked meat. He had been warned that not to eat offered food was, to the Savages, an insult to the one who had offered it, and so he looked for a place where he might dispose of his portion without being seen. Daniel had moved close to the fires, squatting in the Savage fashion, contentedly calling out in the Algonkian tongue to those near him. Laforgue moved into the shadows, going downriver. As he did, a dog ran after him, jumping up, trying to get a scrap of meat. Using this as a solution, he allowed the animal get its teeth into the flesh, then let go of his portion. The dog at once ran off into the undergrowth with its prize.

It rained. A drizzle became a downpour. The fires hissed. Women ran to the canoes to make sure the bundles were covered. The other Savages, ignoring the rain, ate stolidly until the kettles were empty. Then, soaking wet, they entered the night's habitation. Laforgue, sheltering under a tree, saw Neehatin come toward the forest and, turning his good ear in the leader's direction, heard his name.

"Nicanis? Nicanis?"

"Neehatin, you called me?"

"Nicanis, have you eaten?"

"I have truly eaten."

"Then let us go in," Neehatin said. "It will rain all night."

And so, following his host, Laforgue entered the bark habitation, pulling aside the bearskin covering which served as a door. Inside, on the bed of spruce boughs, were huddled all the Savage families, men, women and children, curled in fetal positions or lying on their backs with knees drawn up. Huddled against them or on top of them were their dogs. Laforgue saw Daniel lying in one of these groups, his cloak drawn up to cover his face as though he already slept.

"Here, Nicanis," Neehatin said, pushing aside a woman to make a place for the priest. "Lie there. You will be well."

Obediently Laforgue curled up, his back to an old woman, his face uncomfortably close to a young male who put his arm around the priest as though they were children in the same bed. Dogs crawled over the bodies of the sleepers, looking for a place to lie. A child cried. Two men conversed in low voices. Rain drummed steadily on the birch-bark roof and dripped into the dwelling from a large hole in the top of the habitation which opened on the night sky. The bed of spruce was surprisingly soft and Laforgue buried his face in the boughs, hoping that the smell of the needles would dull the sickly odor of unwashed bodies. He tried, as was his nightly custom, to direct his last waking thoughts to the crucifixion of Jesus. But the old woman behind him kicked him in the back as she rolled over, snoring. The fetid smell of the Savages' breath lay like a low cloud in the confined space, and gradually he became aware of giggles as young girls and boys crawled about in search of each other. He pulled his hat down over his eyes to shut out that which he should not see, but as he did a girl came close to him and he felt his penis stiffen.

How can I sleep in a place like this? I should go out and sleep under the trees. But what about the nights ahead, when the cold will make it impossible to survive outside and alone? This is a test. It is God's wish that I remain here.

Burrowing his face in the branches, he tried to shut out the sound of the lascivious giggles. He began to pray, automatically at first, but at last the words became prayer. *O Lord, I give Thee thanks. Thou hast brought me here.*

▼

Neehatin woke. The dream filled his mind. He did not know what it commanded, but it must be obeyed. The fact that he had dreamed it on the first night of a journey meant it signaled a danger ahead. But what danger? He must divine what it said. He got up and made his way through the mass of sleeping bodies. As he passed his wife, he kicked her in the small of the back, signaling her to rise and follow him. He went out. The sky was quiet. The rain had stopped. Above the forest, the moon watched him as he walked across the clearing. He looked into the forest. The forest was still asleep. He squatted down on the riverbank, facing the waters.

He heard his wife's footsteps in the clearing. In the

Iroquois nation women had power in council, but Nee-hatin's people treated their wives as they did their dogs. Neehatin did not understand why his people behaved thus. His wife had the gift of sight. He looked at her as she came toward him under the gaze of the moon. She was ugly with many winters and bent with the burdens of carrying, cooking and making shelter. Her children did not help her. All were males. When she came up, she squatted down beside him and he knew that she knew. "Yes," he said. "I dreamed."

She looked at him. "On the first night of a journey," she said. "Shit!"

"It's a warning," he said. "That is good, isn't it?"

She did not answer this. "Tell me your dream."

"I was on a log. I paddled across a river and landed in an open place. I walked up to a meadow, and when I did, this fucking big serpent followed me through the grasses."

"Then?"

"I went back to the river and again sat on the log. As I paddled away, a heavy man jumped onto the log behind me and made it rock. I fell in the water and a fish swam up and told me to follow it. It led me to the farther shore. That is all. What does it mean?"

She bent her head, thinking. "The serpent is a sorcerer. We must find a sorcerer to tell us what is the danger."

"So it is a danger, then?"

She nodded. "Yes. The heavy man is the Blackrobe."

Neehatin was surprised. He had not thought of that. "So it is the Blackrobe who brings us danger?"

"Yes."

"But we have taken him with us. What does the dream say I must do?"

"It says you must find the fish. We must get a sorcerer to tell us what is the fish that will save us."

"Mestigoit is a sorcerer," Neehatin said. "He is the only one between here and the winter hunting place. He lives with the Montagnais in the middle place."

"How many nights?"

"Eight."

"Shit," she said. "Eight nights?"

"We will drive hard. With any fucking luck we might do it in seven."

"You must try," she said. She looked at the forest. "The trees have wakened. It is time to go."

"First I must tell the senior men." He looked at her, then at the forest. A great fear came upon him. "I show no fear," he said. He spoke not to his wife but to the forest.

The trees murmured. He did not hear what they said.

"What will I do now?" he asked them.

Smile upon the Blackrobe, the forest said.

"I will do that," Neehatin said.

▼

Laforgue woke. Above him, in the opening of the roof of the Savage habitation, he saw the morning sky. He felt that he would vomit. Shutting his nostrils to the fetid stink of his sleeping companions, he stumbled over to the doorway. When he stepped out into the clearing, all was clean and still. Grass and leaves glittered with dew. In the nearby forest, sunlight struck down through the great aisles of trees, reminding him of the shadows in the nave of the cathedral of Coutances. He looked at the river, at that swift current which carried these waters thousands of leagues to the sea. Near the beached canoes, a small group of Savages squatted in a semicircle, listening to their leader. Laforgue saw Neehatin's lips move but at that distance could not hear what was said. Not wishing to intrude, he walked in the opposite direction, continuing on until he was out of sight of the encampment. Then, alone in the morning silence, he knelt by the current and, undoing the buttons of his cassock, bathed his head and hands in the chill waters. When he had finished he wiped himself dry with tufts of grass, then knelt again to say his morning prayers. As so often, when facing a new trial he invoked the aid of the Virgin Mary.

O Holy Mother, he prayed, I ask for your solemn benediction on this journey. I ask your help in this weakness which has afflicted my ear. Unless this infection abates, I fear I will no longer be able to hear what is told to me. I do not ask your Son to lift this trial from me. I know that these afflictions have a meaning, that God does not allow Himself easily to be conquered and the more one gives, the more one gains, the more one loses, the more one finds. But God sometimes hides Himself, and then the cup is very bitter. When, afflicted by this deafness, I feel unable to carry out His work, I fear in my weakness that He has hidden His face from me. . . .

At that moment a great shadow passed over him, and, looking up, his prayer stillborn on his lips, he saw, high above, a huge eagle of a sort he had never seen in France, its head white, its beak and talons yellow, its great blackish wings rigid as sails, catching the wind eddies as it glided back and forth over the trees. Suddenly, swift as clashing swords, the great wings shut. The eagle plummeted between the trees. And as Laforgue knelt there, his struggles, his deafness, the dangers of this journey were transformed miraculously into a great adventure, a chance to advance God's glory here in a distant land. God was not hidden; He had shown Himself in the eagle's flight. Laforgue saw the eagle rise from the trees, its great wings beating steadily as it carried off its prey. In the beauty of this wild place, his heart sang a *Te Deum* of happiness.

▼

"The other Norman is now awake," Chomina said.

Neehatin, who had just told his dream to the senior men, looked up and saw the boy Iwanchou come across the clearing. Unlike the Blackrobe, this boy had keen ears. Neehatin made a sign of caution to the others. The boy came up.

"When do we leave?" he asked.

"We leave now."

"Good. Nicanis will be pleased."

Neehatin pointed downriver. "Nicanis is awake and went down there. Find him and tell him we are ready."

"I will do that," the boy said.

The senior men watched him go. "Why did you say we will leave?" one of them asked. "There is good hunting here."

"Because the dream says we must."

"Are you sure of that?" asked Ougebemat, an old man who, years ago, had fought with Agnonha against the Iroquois. The senior man turned to him. Ougebemat was one who read dreams.

"I am sure," Neehatin said, but he felt the sweat of fear trickle from the hair at his neck.

"The man who made you fall off the log is the Blackrobe," Ougebemat said. "Am I right?"

Neehatin looked at him, alarmed. He says what my wife said. "Yes, you are right," Neehatin said.

"Then to obey the dream we should leave these Norman pigs and go on alone."

Neehatin shook his head. "It does not tell me that. Besides, we have made a promise to their leader. Do you not fear his anger, you who fought beside him?"

"I shit upon his anger. I shit upon all Normans," Ougebemat said. "I fear the dream."

"I, too, fear it," Neehatin said. "And I obey it by taking these Norman turds in our canoes. The dream told me that the serpent is a sorcerer, and so we must keep the Blackrobe with us until the sorcerer tells us what to do with him."

He saw at once that his words had won the argument. There was agreement among the senior men. If the dream said the serpent was a sorcerer, then Ougebemat was overruled.

"If the dream tells you that," Ougebemat said, "then it must be obeyed. For it is not dreamed by some useless prick, but by a leader."

The others made the sound of approval, for of course Ougebemat spoke the truth. The dream of a leader must be obeyed. A dream is more real than death or battle.

"We must leave at once," Neehatin said. "The sorcerer, Mestigoit, is seven nights, maybe eight, from here. We will be in danger until we find him. We must travel as if there is a fire at our back. Agreed?"

All gave the guttural of assent. They rose. The parley was over. Neehatin felt the muscles of his neck tremble with tension and pulled his chin down lest Chomina notice, Chomina who watched other men as a hunter watches for a movement which will tell him when to strike. But Chomina did not know that the dream had told Neehatin nothing, that it was Neehatin's wife who said the serpent meant a sorcerer.

And at that moment, aware that—while these men did not know he had not spoken the truth—the river, the forest, the animals they would hunt all knew his lie, Neehatin looked again at the forest and felt great fear. And again the forest spoke, reassuring him. *Smile upon the Blackrobe*, the forest said.

I have done so, Neehatin told the trees. He turned and signaled to the women who had come up. "Take down the birch bark. Load the canoes. Hurry."

3

In the next four days, the Savages paddled from dawn to dusk. They did not stop to eat or even to relieve themselves; to Laforgue's disgust, while in the canoes they urinated into the kettles used for cooking food. When Laforgue wished to defecate, the Algonkin who acted as lead paddler in his canoe signaled him to do so off the rear of the craft. And so, in shame among the gibes of the children and to the amusement of the women, he must bare his buttocks to the wind. The Savages, foul-mouthed as always, called out jokes and insults, some of which he did not catch, but those he heard made him wince; one woman yelling, "Look at his white bum," and another, "Show us your prick, Nicanis"; and yet, with all this banter, their paddling did not cease and the canoe was not allowed to fall behind the others. The Savages' strength amazed him; they paddled in relays, never shirking their turn. His shoulders ached and his arms felt as though they had been wrenched on a rack. But he remembered Father Brabant's warning: "When you take up a paddle in their canoes, do not lay it down until you have done your share. If you do, they will despise you." And so, hour after hour, in pain, he toiled with them, smiling as they insulted him. There was no harm in these insults. They insulted each other ceaselessly but did not take offense. In Québec, when he had first studied their language, he had been warned by Father Bourque of their habit of answering questions about the word "God" or "heaven" by giving as the equivalent some foul word like fuck or cunt. And so, said Father Bourque, we must be constantly on guard against this and learn well all the filthy words they employ. Now, to his shame, these words were often the only part of a Savage sentence which made sense to his failing ears.

Each night at the onset of darkness, the canoes landed. A fire was lit and the foul corn gruel called sagamité was cooked over an open fire. It tasted, to Laforgue, like watery glue, yet he must eat it or starve. The Savages no longer thought of hunting. When they had eaten, they crept into the night's makeshift habitation and slept until the hour before dawn, when they rose, ate some of the cold sagamité left over from the night before and, collecting their belongings, knelt again in the canoe. Laforgue and Daniel, although weary and often faint, quickly accustomed themselves to this rhythm of travel and, like the Algonkin, passed the day mainly in silence, paddling, staring at the lank hair and tawny shoulders of the paddler ahead, traveling through landscapes which, hour after hour, day after day, never seemed to change.

On the evening of the fourth day, shortly before the canoes landed for the night, it began to rain. The Algonkin, on landing, at once put on the garments they wore in cold weather, long tunics and stockings made of moose skin which they tied around them with many thongs. Laforgue, stiff from his day's work, stumbled and fell as he came up the riverbank. Daniel at once ran to him.

"Are you all right, Father Paul?"

Laforgue smiled. "Even though I was trained to kneel for hours in the chapel, it seems I have lost the habit."

As he and Daniel went on they saw, in a small knot near the trees, Chomina, Neehatin and the senior men, a strange sight in their moose-skin garments, their heads close in a parley. Neehatin turned and looked at the priest. His lips moved.

"He is calling you," Daniel said. "Do you not hear him?"

"Yes, yes, I hear him," Laforgue said, but saw only that the Savage moved his lips.

"Come with me," Laforgue told Daniel. "You can help me speak with him."

Neehatin came toward them in the rain, saying something Laforgue could not catch.

"What does he say?"

"He says they have paddled hard so that we will reach the rapids early, as Agnonha wishes. He asks that you give them thank-yous."

"Thank-yous?"

"It's the word they use when they want you to give them a gift."

"What thank-yous do you want?" Laforgue said to the leader.

"You have tobacco," Neehatin said. "We do not. With tobacco we will paddle hard and you will be pleased."

"But we are keeping the tobacco to trade on the Ottawa."

Neehatin smiled. It was not a pleasant smile. *"Khisakhiran,"* he said.

Khisakhiran was a phrase the Savages used to criticize the French for not sharing with others. *Khisakhiran* meant "You love it, you love it more than us." The Savages shared everything, even with strangers. But Laforgue remembered the Superior's warning: "If you give to them what you have, they will ask and ask until they have taken all you own."

"What if I give a pipeful to each?" Laforgue asked Neehatin, smiling to show he was not offended at the insult.

But the Algonkin shook his head and said contemptuously, *"Sakhita."* It meant, "Since you love it, then love it." He walked away.

"He is offended, Father."

"I know he is offended. I am not deaf."

"If we do not share with them," Daniel said, "how can we expect them to share with us?"

Laforgue felt himself flush. Why is it that this boy, barely twenty, feels he can lecture me on how to deal with the Savages? "All right," he said angrily. He called after Neehatin. "Neehatin, forgive me. Please take the tobacco."

The Savage stopped, then turned around, staring at Laforgue. Inexplicably, he burst into laughter.

"I am sorry," Laforgue said again.

"We will smoke," Neehatin said and smiled. He called to the women. "Get the tobacco from Nicanis's canoe. Now we will truly smoke."

Two young girls ran down to Laforgue's canoe and began to undo one of the bundles. "It's the wrong bundle," Laforgue said to Daniel. "What if they find the altar wine?"

At once, Daniel ran to the canoe and, laughing, slapped a tall slender girl, who was undoing the bundle which contained vestments, missals and the altar wine. Laughing, the girl hit Daniel, who caught hold of her and pulled her to the bundle in which the tobacco was stored. Neehatin walked down to the canoe and took possession of the small bale of tobacco which Laforgue had counted on to help them pay the Allumette people for their help in portages on the upper river. A cry of joy went up.

The priest turned, walked away and, under the shelter of the trees, took out his breviary. The rain had almost ceased. As he read his office, his weariness was such that his eyes closed and he fell asleep. When he woke, the fires were lit and the cooked sagamité was being apportioned. The men and the older women lay around smoking their pipes. Laforgue pulled his cloak around him. He was hungry, but the thought of sagamité repelled him. He rose and, taking his knife, began to cut some spruce branches and arrange them in a pallet under the shelter of a large tree. As he did, someone came toward him in the darkness. It was Daniel.

"What are you doing, Father Paul?"

"I thought I would sleep out here for a change."

"Why?"

"I have trouble with my sleep in the habitation. The stink, the noise, the things that go on in there."

"What things?" Daniel stared at the priest.

"Have you not seen? Better you should not. I am not happy that you sleep there either. Especially you."

"Why especially me?"

"The Savages are like dogs. They have no—" He felt himself flush. These were things he did not want to put into words.

"But we cannot sleep outside," Daniel said. "It may rain again. If we fall sick, the Algonkin will not help us."

"They would not leave us."

"But they would not help us. We must fend for ourselves. That is their way. And something is wrong. Haven't you noticed?"

"Wrong?"

"Why are we traveling like this? I heard Chomina's wife say that we must travel like this for three more days."

"Merciful God," Laforgue said. "Can we stand it?"

"We must," the boy said. "Besides, it's what you wanted, isn't it? You told me we are late in starting on the journey."

"By my map," Laforgue said, "in three days we should reach the first falls. Perhaps that is what they have in mind."

"I don't know," the boy said. "But they are worried about something. Look, it's raining again. Let's go in."

And so, in company with Daniel, Laforgue entered the stinking habitation. Within minutes dogs scrambled over him, walking on his stomach. He struck out, crying, *"Aché, aché,"* the words the Savages used to drive dogs off, but it was useless. The Savages did not feed their animals in any regular manner, and these last days, with no hunting, there were no scraps and so, hungry and restless, the dogs stuck their snouts in and out among the sleeping bodies. A child bawled. Laforgue drew his cloak over his face and covered his ears with his hands. As on previous nights, his whole body ached with grievous pain. I will never be able to sleep.

And, at once, he fell asleep.

▼

When he woke again it was pitch dark. He uncovered his face and looked up at the opening which showed the sky. The moon had hidden itself. The habitation now slept the sleep of the predawn hour, the Savages huddled in a cohesive mass, like some great animal, twitching as though dreaming a collective dream. Laforgue moved stiffly, his shoulders in pain from his labors in the canoe. As he did, he saw that Daniel was no longer his sleepmate. In Daniel's place a Savage woman lay, her face within inches of his, her mouth open, her breathing sonorous in a fluttering snore. Laforgue squirmed around and sat up, looking for Daniel. But in the darkness it was impossible to tell one body from another. Again he was nauseated by the smell. Perhaps Daniel went outside? Laforgue rose and, stumbling, trying not to walk on others, made his way to the flap which screened off the entrance.

Outside the night air was fresh as new wine. The great silence, the immensity of the sky, the clean smell of the forest, all were the delicious obverse of the cramped, fetid habitation. Above, amid trailing leaves of cloud, the moon slipped in and out of sight like some plump, mysterious fruit, its cold rays lighting the dark floor of the forest in a steely sheen. He looked around. He was alone.

Slowly, he walked across the open space and faced the river's current. The night was warm. It was as though, after the rain, the summer's heat had stolen back. He turned, half tempted to go and make his bed there among the trees. And then, so close as to make the skin prickle on his neck, a man's voice spoke softly in the Savage tongue. A second voice murmured a reply. His heart pounded. He remembered the Superior's warning about the suddenness of the enemy. They were speaking to each other. They had not seen him. The sound came from directly behind him, in the trees. Bending down foolishly in a half crouch, as though by diminishing his height he lessened his chance of being seen, he turned to face the forest.

He heard new sounds. It was no longer speech but a kind of moaning. He heard, also, the rustle of undergrowth. Moving forward he gently parted a screen of birch leaves and was instantly in full view of two people. But they did not see him.

He crouched down, half closing the screen of leaves but still peering through. He heard himself begin to pant, his breathing an imitation of the sounds ahead. The moonlight slipped clear of all cloud, shining bright as day. He stared at the naked forms, the boy kneeling behind the girl, his hands gripping her waist, the girl bent over, her arms and face on the ground, as he came into her from behind, like dogs coupling. The boy lifted his head as his loins thrust into her. His face was wild with excitement. The boy was Daniel. The moaning sounds were his.

And Laforgue, peering through the leaves, saw it all, saw her nakedness, her pointed breasts almost touching the ground, her face contorted as though in pain. And as he saw it he tried to still his own agitation. He watched and watched, afraid of being seen, his mind flooded with this vision of lust. He felt his penis swell and stiffen until it hurt. He moved his head a little, peering in, not wanting to miss the next thrust of the boy's loins. And to his shock and excitement it was as though he were the boy, rearing above that Savage girl, the same girl he had seen earlier, the tall slim girl who had run down to get tobacco from the canoe.

The boy gasped in climax, then leaned forward, resting his head on her shoulders. Both eased down onto the improvised nest they had fashioned from branches and clothing. He watched as, slowly, the girl's fingers began to move along Daniel's thigh. She raised herself up and then, to Laforgue's astonishment, her head moved down to his loins. In all his celibate dreams, dreams for which he had scourged himself in his novice cell, he had never imagined such a thing. The girl kissed and sucked on Daniel's penis, and the sight filled him with such a mixture of shame, anger and desire that he felt he would faint. The girl crawled around in the makeshift bed and now, as she kissed Daniel in that place, she presented her narrow girlish buttocks to the Jesuit's avid stare, as though offering him the same delight she had just given to the boy.

And at that, as though possessed, Laforgue began to

fumble with the buttons of his cassock. Kneeling, still staring, his breathing harsh as a tearing sheet, he began to jerk furiously until his semen spurted, spilling on the ground. The lovers, kissing each other, began again to rear up, positioning themselves for coitus as their watcher turned away, crawling clumsily on all fours, moving in awkward haste across the clearing until he was close to the riverbank. He rose and, stumbling, in panic, began to run. He ran down the riverbank and along the edge of the current, running until the encampment was far out of sight.

He stopped and looked back. He was alone. It was as though he were the only living thing in this place. He bowed his head and began to sob, in a harsh broken rhythm, the sound oddly loud as it echoed across the moonlit waters of the river. He stood sobbing in that wild place, bereft of all hope, beyond all forgiveness. The moon faded, and gradually a bloody dawn was born in the sky. Laforgue turned away from the river and, taking out his knife, went again into the forest, coming back with some spruce boughs, trimmed and pliant, twisted to form a discipline. Again he faced the river, then lowered his cassock and unbuttoned his undershirt, leaving his torso bare. Methodically, as though he used a flail on wheat, he scourged his back, lash after lash, as blood spilt into the folds of his lowered robe, until his flayed back was purpled as the sky above. Only then did he cast the discipline aside and, falling to his knees, try to say the prayers of penance, the prayers of shame.

▼

"Where is Nicanis?" Neehatin called, as the canoes were placed in the water.

Daniel looked around. Where was he? And then he saw the priest come around the bend of the riverbank, walking slowly, as though in thought. "Father Laforgue?" Laforgue looked up and, seeing the Algonkin ready to depart, hurried to join them. Where had he been? Daniel wondered, but then lost interest in the priest for there *she* was, getting into Chomina's canoe, kneeling behind her mother as they moved out into the stream. Daniel paddled, trying to come closer to her, but his paddlers stalled the canoe in the water, signaling him to wait. There was a rule to travel. First Neehatin's canoe, then Chomina's. Then the others. As she passed she did not look at him. He knew she would not look at him. Nor did she want him to look at her. Oonta had told him that was their custom. A suitor must pretend no interest in the girl; he must not look at her or speak to her or stay near her, unless accidentally. Otherwise everyone will make a mockery of him and the girl will feel shame for him.

Look at me, he willed her as her canoe glided by. Your canoe will be ahead of mine all day. I will not see you until night.

If she does not want me to look at her, it means she sees me as a suitor. But that's impossible. The Algonkin don't care if we sleep with their girls, but they will never accept me as her husband. They say we are ugly and hairy, that we do not share with others as they do. They believe themselves to be more intelligent than we are.

Yet she *must* see me as a suitor. Otherwise she would laugh and look at me as the other girls do. Oonta and that other little girl at the eel fishery let me do what I wanted. They did not care if I looked at them and spoke to them when others were present. But she does. She tells me I am not ugly as are the other French. Yet she let Mercier put his prick inside her. She kissed him there.

I cannot bear to think of that. When I was fourteen and in the schoolyard of the Récollet Fathers, I saw a boy pass around filthy drawings to the others. I gave him all my money so that I could take the drawings and tear them up. That is how I feel when I think of her and Mercier. Yet why do I feel that way, when I myself think of doing it to her, all day, all night? I am now the opposite of the boy in the schoolyard, the boy I once was.

Does she think of me as a suitor? What would Chomina say? I think he likes me; he says he loves me well. But one cannot believe what they say. They lie to us as they would never lie to each other, because they do not think of us as men but as monsters. Father Bourque said when they first saw our ships and went aboard, we offered them wine and dry biscuit. They went back and told their people that we were devils who lived in a floating wooden island and drank blood and ate dry bones. They believe animals have souls and intelligence. They believe the trees are alive and watching them. Because we do not believe as they do, they think us stupid. They would only accept me if I became as they are. They might adopt me then, as they do some of their prisoners. But Father Bourque said they rarely adopt their prisoners: instead they torture and kill them. To become one of them I would have to torture and kill as they do.

Could I? I have tortured my Savior, and for a girl who is not a girl but a wild animal. I give her presents, yes, but it is not just for presents that she sleeps with me. She thinks of me as a suitor. It must be that.

What do I know? I cannot think. I no longer pray, I who once wanted to give my life for God. I think I am in love with her, but how can it be love when it will bring me eternal damnation? If I died tonight I would go straight to hell. Yet even though I know it, I cannot repent. I cannot because I do not wish to lose her. To save my soul I should at once confess to Father Paul. But if I did, he would make it his duty to keep me away from her. I must have her. I will have her tonight. I will be damned for all eternity. She thinks of me as her suitor. I think only of that.

▼

On the sixth day of the race to the sorcerer, it turned cold. High gray clouds dulled the sky as the canoes sped along the great concourse of the river. The Savages pressed on as never before. Even when, ahead of the leading canoe, a family of moose blundered down to the water—the male raising its antlered head to utter a cry of alarm, the females stock-still in the shallows—Neeha-tin's arm rose in signal, commanding the paddlers to continue.

The rain ceased. Just before dark, soft drifting snowflakes fell like a swarm of moths. Laforgue, his back smarting from his self-inflicted contrition, looked up at the sky. At once he thought of the aide-mémoire written for him by the Superior:

*If a heavy snowfall occurs within two weeks of the
start of your journey, the Algonkin may decide not to
travel farther but to winter in some place where they
can hunt large animals who flounder in the snow. I
pray that the snows will not come until you have passed
the rapids. It is there the portages are the longest. I
must warn you that in the past Father Brabant and Father Gulot were left below the rapids with one canoe
and little food, but they still reached their destination
with the help of this map. God did not turn from them
as He will not turn from you. Your journey is in His
hands.*

But this is not a true snowfall, Laforgue reflected as
he stared into the mist of snowflakes. And if we are
abandoned by the Savages, at least Daniel will be removed from the occasion of sin. What am I to do? It is
my duty to ask him to confess and abjure the company of
that girl. But how can I speak to him? Who am I to speak
to anyone, I who am unspeakable?

When the canoes landed, the snow was thick on the
ground. Neehatin called out instructions about the habitation, instructions Laforgue did not hear because at that
moment he was looking for Daniel. Where was he, was
he with that girl? He went to the place where the women
were cutting boughs for the habitation and saw the girl
with two others, dragging spruce branches out of the forest. As was the custom, while they worked they exchanged foul words and insults, laughing all the while.
When Laforgue looked at her face he felt his cheeks grow
warm with embarrassment.

The girl's long black hair was gathered behind her
neck and held in place by a disk of native copper. She

wore a necklace of beads which fell between her breasts. Like so many of the Savages her skin was light, as though bronzed by the sun, and her teeth were gleaming white. But her tunic, as was usual, was greasy and stained and her arms and legs were blackened with grime from the campfires. He looked at her and had to force himself to look away. *The devil uses her against us.*

At that moment he saw Daniel come from the forest, his cap filled with wild berries. Daniel came up to him at once.

"Here, Father. Take some."

As Laforgue took a handful he avoided Daniel's eye. Into his mind came the lustful picture that, last night, he had tried to burn into his brain. In silence, he ate the bitter berries.

"How was the day?" the boy asked.

He shrugged awkwardly. He did not feel able to speak. *If I speak, I must confront him.*

"Something is very wrong," Daniel said.

"Wrong?" Laforgue's voice was hoarse.

"One of the Savages told me they must reach a certain place by tomorrow night. I don't know why."

"A Savage told you? Which one?"

"Chomina's daughter," the boy said. His face showed no concern.

"That one? That girl over there? The one dragging branches?"

Daniel looked to where the three girls were working. "Yes, the tall one," he said. He kept looking at the girl. "They will build a winter habitation tonight," he said. "It's because of the snow."

I must speak to him. I must tell him that I know.

But, as before, he could not say the words. Instead, he reached into Daniel's cap and took a few more of the bitter berries. As he munched them, Daniel turned and went across the clearing to where the men were using their snowshoes as shovels to clear a space for the habitation. The tall girl, laughing, began to call out something to the others. Nearby, the older women were cooking the night's meal of sagamité, pushing long branches into the blazing fire.

Laforgue turned away. Tears filled his eyes, tears he did not understand. He went into the woods and, stumbling, found a place where the snow had not fallen. There, under the trees, he knelt to pray. Tears wet his cheeks as he said, over and over, the words of contrition. *O my God, I am heartily sorry for having offended Thee.* His lips moved but, even as he prayed, the image of last night came into his mind and his penis stiffened. He knelt there for a long time. The darkness came. He heard someone call his name.

"Father Paul?"

He rose and came out of the tree shelter. Daniel stood in the clearing. "Have you eaten?"

"I am not hungry," Laforgue said.

"Neehatin wants us to go in. We will leave at first light."

Because of the cold the habitation was smaller than those built before, and with a lower roof. The Savages must crawl in on hands and knees. A fire burned in its center and the smoke was suffocating, blinding the eyes and causing everyone to cough. Laforgue's nose and throat were assailed in such force by the smoke that he pressed his face into the spruce branches on the ground.

Despite the fierce heat of the fire his back froze. In the noise of the coughing and the crying of children, sleep was impossible. Daniel lay near him but when, after a while, Laforgue opened his eyes he could no longer see in the haze. He lay, his mind shipwrecked among snatches of prayer, anguished promises that he would confront the boy, and the troubling and insidious images of lust which again came before him. At last when, the fire dying and the smoke abating, he sensed all were asleep, he managed to raise himself up and peer about for Daniel. But as he had feared the boy was nowhere to be seen. Crawling about amid the grumbles of sleepy Savages, Laforgue at last reached the bearskin which served as a door and, on his hands and knees, came out into the open. The night air was very cold. The moon was not visible. He could barely see ten paces in front of him. As he stood up, a roaring filled his infected ear and for a moment he thought he would lose consciousness. The moon came out from behind a cloud so that, for the first time, he could see his path. He entered the forest. He did not call out Daniel's name, and as he moved cautiously in the undergrowth he realized, with shame, that he had wished to come on them unseen. And if I do, if I see them copulating, will I hide and again become the third actor in this scene? I am not competent to counsel or censure him. I am no longer fit to be a priest.

He turned and left the forest. The night was now freezing cold. At the door of the habitation he crawled in, burrowing himself a place among a huddle of sleeping Savages. At last, warmed by human contact, exhausted, he fell asleep.

4

The savages sang. They had been singing since dawn, when they embarked on the river. Their songs were, as always, monotonous chants, without gaiety, attuned to the rhythm of their labors. But this was the first time they had sung in seven days. It was as though the song were a celebration, as though the journey were ending. And indeed, shortly after noon, on a sudden signal from Neehatin, the paddling ceased. As the canoes drifted on the edge of the current, a loon skimmed low over the waters, uttering its lonely call. In the silence which followed, Neehatin seemed to listen. And then, from the trees by the shoreline, some twenty unknown Savages came, waving aloft their javelins and shields. From their dress and decorations they seemed similar to the Algonkin, and at sight of them Neehatin sent his canoes toward shore. As the canoes came in, some of the strangers ran into the shallows, helping to lift them to dry land. Laforgue leaned forward, clumsily rocking his craft. "Who are these?" he asked.

"Montagnais," said his paddler.

As the Savages had no way of greeting strangers, their greeting was simply to accept the strangers' help in disembarking from their craft. The newcomers were all male. When Daniel and Laforgue stepped ashore these men came up, circling them as though they were strange sights. At last, one of the newcomers turned to Ougebemat. "Why does this one wear black stuff?"

"Because he is a fucking demon," Ougebemat said, and some of the Algonkin began to laugh.

"They are covered with hair like a pig," a newcomer said. "Why did you bring us these ugly pigs?"

"Because they are hungry," Ougebemat said. "They wanted to eat us, but we told them they would have to eat you instead. We told them you are shit and you taste sweet."

All were laughing now, Algonkin and Montagnais, but Laforgue, watching, could see that some of the newcomers were still uneasy. He smiled at them and said, "We have come to help you. We are sent by our great God, who is the God of all of us, even of you whom we have never seen."

"This black one cannot speak properly. He barks like a dog," a Montagnais said.

"They are Normans and they also speak their own tongue, which is like birds singing," Chomina said.

"They are strange ones. They live on wooden islands in the great water. They are ugly, all right, but they have good presents to give. And we love them because their leader Agnonha fought and won for us, many winters ago, when we killed the fucking Iroquois."

"Then they are Agnonha's men," said one of the newcomers. "They are the shits who love furs."

"They love them more than life," Chomina said, and all laughed.

Neehatin then raised his hand. "Is Mestigoit with you?"

"He is."

"Good. I must speak with him." He turned to his group. "Look for berries and game. I will be back soon."

"There is no hunting in this part," one of the newcomers said. "We are moving on."

"Yesterday we saw moose," Chomina said.

"That was yesterday, you shithead," the newcomer said, laughing. "If you stay here I'll tell you what you will eat. You will eat tree bark."

Neehatin approached Laforgue. "I will not be long, Nicanis. There is someone I must see before we move on."

The newcomers went with him. All disappeared in the trees. "Tell me," Daniel asked Laforgue. "Have you thought what you will do if they abandon us?"

"We will go on alone. But why would they abandon us?"

Daniel did not answer. He took up his musket. "I'll go into the forest," he said. "Maybe I can find some game." He went off. Some of the Algonkian males took their spears and hatchets and also went into the woods.

Laforgue looked at the tall girl, who was picking fleas from her mother's hair and eating them. The Savages ate these insects, not from appetite but as a revenge against the fleas for having been bitten by them. That was what Father Bourque had told him. He said it was part of their feelings toward their enemies. An enemy must be shown no mercy. He must be crushed. Laforgue sat down, opened his breviary and began to read his daily office. When he had finished, some children ran up and snatched off his wide-brimmed hat. Running after them to retrieve it, he stumbled and fell.

As he got up, wincing because he had bruised his knee, he saw Neehatin come from the forest, followed by a small figure which, at first, Laforgue took to be a child. But this was no child. It was the only deformed Savage he had yet seen, a small hunchback, his wizened face painted a bright yellow, a strange pigtailed hat perched on his naked skull. He wore an extraordinary garment of old patched fur and carried a loose bag of skins containing his belongings. When the women and children saw this figure, they fell silent. Neehatin, crossing the clearing, made a sign to Chomina, who had not gone into the woods. Chomina got up and, entering the forest, uttered a loud high cry which imitated some animal. It was a signal for the hunters to return. The hunchback, meantime, walked around the clearing, peering at the faces of the women and children like an actor taking his bow, but stopped abruptly when he reached Laforgue. His glittering black eyes narrowed and blinked as though he faced a blinding light. He turned and looked to Neehatin, who nodded, whereupon the hunchback, stepping carefully as though he trod on river ice, moved very close to the

Jesuit. Laforgue, holding his wide-brimmed hat in one hand, his breviary in the other, smiled uncertainly at the little man who now stood directly beneath him, immobile, looking up, his painted face dead as a mask, its only sign of life his glittering jewel eyes. There was something about him which caused Laforgue an instant unease so that, forgetting what he had been taught about addressing a strange Savage, he said, "I am Nicanis. What is your name?"

"Ah! Ah! Ah!" The hunchback danced up and down in a sudden rage. "Why do you tell your name? Why do you ask my name? You know you must never do that."

"I am sorry," Laforgue said. "I forgot." For it was true that the Savages did not like to be asked their names and, if asked, would pretend not to understand. Father Bourque had told him, also, that he should not tell his own name unasked.

He stared at the little hunchback, who continued to dance up and down, calling, "Ah! Ah! Ah!" as though he were in pain.

"I said I am sorry." Laforgue tried to smile. "I ask your pardon."

"No, no, no," the hunchback cried. "You lie. I will tell you why you said that name. Because it is not your name. It is the name of the man who was in your body before you crept inside it. You are not Nicanis, whoever that man was. You are a demon."

Laforgue felt himself start. "Why do you say that?" he asked.

"Because *I* am a demon," the hunchback said. "Oh, yes. Everyone knows it. I entered the cunt of an Algonkian woman thirty winters past and was borne by her as a child. And you, Blackrobe, you also are a demon. Now, let me see." He turned away from Laforgue, half bowing, again circling like an actor before his audience. He stopped, facing the forest, and waited, in a pose of total immobility.

At that moment, as though in a play, Chomina's hunters came from the trees. Among them was Daniel. The hunchback pointed to Daniel. For a moment all was still, the figures in the clearing frozen as figures in a frieze.

"Let me look at you," the hunchback cried. "Are you this demon's son? Are you? No, no, I see it now. You are just another Norman pig, a greedy fucker in love with furs."

Daniel smiled. "I am not in love with furs. I am here to help this Father in his work. We are traveling north to the country of the Hurons."

"Father, what Father?" the hunchback shouted, as though he misunderstood. "This Blackrobe is not your Father, I tell you. He is not what he says he is. He is a demon." He bent over, opened his bag of skins and took from it a drum of the sort used by the Savages for their ceremonies and songs, a flat circular drum made of skins with pebbles inside it. He held up the drum and, circling again, shook it as he made his way back to Laforgue. He shook the drum to the right of the Jesuit, then to the left. He began to howl in a loud ferocious manner and ran around Laforgue, still shaking the drum. The Savages stood silent, watching. At the third circling, the hunchback laid down his drum in front of the priest, then, turning, scuttled back across the clearing to Neehatin, who bent to listen as the little man whispered in his ear. When he had finished, the hunchback ran back and picked up the drum. He no longer looked at Laforgue. It was as though the priest had ceased to exist.

"He is a sorcerer," Daniel said to Laforgue.

A sorcerer. Laforgue thought of what Father Brabant had written in the *Relations*.

The sorcerers are our greatest enemies. They are cunning and prey on the people's ignorance. But, also, in some way I fear that they may traffic with the devil. I do not know for sure, but when I traveled with the Savages, the sorcerer did his best to impede my efforts to implant the Faith. I felt he was the agent of the Evil One. Day and night he incited others to kill me.

Neehatin raised his hand. "We will go now," he told the band. "Mestigoit will travel in the canoe of Nicanis. We will find moose upriver. My dream tells me so."

And now, as the canoes slid into the water, the children and the sorcerer climbed into the center of Laforgue's craft. The hunchback arranged himself with his back to the forward paddlers, his legs drawn up underneath him in a squatting position, his glittering eyes fixed on Laforgue, as though he were his jailer. Laforgue, made uneasy by this stare, heard again the strange words of the hunchback. *You are not Nicanis, whoever that man was. You are a demon.* Can it be that this man is the devil's agent and sees the mark of my sin in me? Or can it be that the Evil One is using him to tempt me to despair and doubt and so prevent me from completing my mission?

Now that they had found the sorcerer, the Savages no longer seemed driven. After less than two hours they disembarked in a long meadow, fringed by the omnipresent trees of the forest. At once, Neehatin gave permission to the hunters to go in search of game, while the women, as usual, began to build a habitation. It had not snowed here, but the air was chill.

Laforgue sat alone, reading his breviary, but as he did, he saw the hunchback Mestigoit urinating at the far end of the meadow. He and Laforgue were the only men left in camp. The sorcerer came up and sat cross-legged in front of the priest as Laforgue turned the pages of his breviary. From his bag of skins the sorcerer took his flat drum and shook it. After a few moments he began to howl, accompanying his strange cries with a frantic rattling of the drum. The noise caused Laforgue's head to ring, but he read on. Seeing this, the sorcerer rose and began to dance around the Jesuit, stamping his feet, shaking the drum close to Laforgue's face, howling so horribly that there could no longer be any pretense of ignoring him.

Laforgue shut his breviary. "What's wrong?" he asked. "Why do you do this?"

The hunchback stopped prancing and put his head on one side. "I am driving you out, demon. I am telling you to come out of that man's body and leave this place. You fear noise, demon. You do not like the drum."

"I am not a demon," Laforgue said, whereupon the hunchback shook his drum, resumed his howling cries and danced up and down as before. Laforgue, trying to control his anger, put his breviary in his cassock pocket and walked across the meadow, going toward the woods.

The woods were dangerous. Father Bourque warned that if you did not track your path exactly you could become lost as in a maze. But as he heard the sorcerer's drum at his back, Laforgue entered the forest, penetrating farther and farther into the aisles of trees. As he hurried on, the hunchback's howls grew fainter until, at last, he could no longer hear them. He stopped to listen and heard, far away, the rattling sound of the drum. He went on.

At last there was silence. He looked around. On every side, the forest was the same. Long shafts of light struck down from a great height, increasing the gloom. There was no wind. He decided to remain here until the pestilential hunchback had found some other diversion. He sat down with his back to a tree and looked up at the sky. The afternoon seemed endless. As he gazed around at the undergrowth and its carpet of leaves and mosses, the thought came to him that in this great empty land, so few Savages roamed the woods that he could be the first man in all history to walk into this particular glade.

As this thought struck him, he realized that he did not know which way he had come. Where was the meadow? He looked again at the sky, but the sky gave no clue. He remembered Father Bourque's advice. "If you are lost, do not try to walk out blindly." Surely he was only minutes away from the place where the Savages had beached their canoes. He thought of the hunchback. Perhaps the hunchback was close? He called out, "Mestigoit? Mestigoit, answer me. Sound your drum." But his words echoed as in a cave. He looked left, then right. I will be calm. I will wait quietly until I hear the hunters returning. I may even see them, here among the trees. But what if they do not come back in this direction? Surely they will send men to look for me. I will pray. It may be that the Lord has chosen for me to end here alone in this wilderness. If that be Thy will, I am Thy servant and I give Thee thanks. But even as he prayed he knew that he did not give thanks. Instead, he was gripped by a growing, blinding fear.

He listened again, but all was so still that he asked himself if his failing right ear had now become totally deaf. He stood up, taking a branch, and struck it against the base of a tree. He heard, clearly, the sound it made. Why is it so quiet? I cannot be more than a quarter of a mile from the meadow. If I move off in this direction and walk for a quarter of a mile and do not find the meadow, I will retrace my steps to this point.

He began to walk, looking down to see if he left tracks. But the leafy undergrowth recorded no imprint. He then used a small branch to score a mark on every third tree and in this way went what seemed to be a quarter of a mile. The sky was darker now. He wondered if he could climb a tree and seek out his bearings. But these trees, tall, with few lower branches, seemed unclimbable. He decided, all at once, that he was going deeper into the forest, moving away from the meadow. He started back. For the first few minutes he managed to retrace his steps by means of the markers, but then, he did not know why, he could no longer find any markers. He was lost.

"Mestigoit? Mestigoit? This is Nicanis." But no one

heard. Or perhaps the hunchback lurked somewhere in the trees listening, the hunchback who was a sorcerer in league with the devil, a sorcerer who believed him a demon and would be glad to let him die. He felt sweat on his brow. "Mestigoit?" he called. "Mestigoit, the demon has left me. Help me."

The sky was very dark. It was the edge of night. The hunters would have returned by now. *Daniel will ask Neehatin to send out men to look for me. But if the sorcerer says I am a demon and have fled into the woods, perhaps Neehatin will not send men to find me. I must be calm. De profundis clamavi ad te, Dominum. Out of the depths have I cried unto Thee, O Lord. O Lord, hear my voice.*

Suddenly, he heard a shout. It was the most wonderful sound. His heart hammered. He listened, but again all was silence. *I cannot have imagined it. It was a shout.*

He set off, hurrying in the direction of the shout. Or *was* it the direction? He must be calm, but he ran faster, stumbling, panting, peering amid the dappled gloom of the trees. "Chomina?" he called. "Chomina, it's Nicanis." *Perhaps he was going in the wrong direction.* He stopped. His breath sounded spent as though he would collapse. *To be so near, yet to miss them. If they had moved on, he might never catch up with them.* Again he began to run, but now at an angle to his previous direction, his eyes straining to discern the shapes of men in the gloom of trees, his dulled ears waiting a further shout.

Terror. He gasped as if he had been struck a mortal blow. Ahead of him, like a flashing blur of darkness, a

Savage, his spear uplifted, rushed through the trees to kill him. The spear was almost in his chest when the Savage face opened in a grin. "Shit!" the Savage cried. "I thought I had a moose but all I have is this silly prick, Nicanis." At once, three other Savages materialized like ghosts in the murk of trees.

"I am lost," Laforgue told them.

"Come, then," the Savage said. "We are going back to the habitation. Why did you come in here, if you do not know the woods?"

"He's an old woman," a second Savage said, laughing. "The woods are for men."

The Savages, surrounding him, laughed and laughed. Laforgue began to laugh as well. Never had their foul banter amused him until now. Moved in some way he did not understand, he embraced the Savage who had found him, burying his face in the filthy tunic which covered the man's torso. And as he did, his laughter changed to tears. I might have died here, alone in this wilderness. I did not welcome death, as a holy person should. I was afraid.

"What is wrong with you, you silly prick?" the Savage asked. "Why are you weeping? Come on. Let's go back."

He shivered. Like a dog behind its masters, he stumbled in their wake as they moved swiftly through the trackless woods, ignoring the darkness around them. On and on they went, laughing, making their foul jokes, abusing each other as they had abused him until, suddenly, ahead he saw a distant blaze of flame. They emerged into the long meadow. The habitation had been built, the fires were lit. The Savages with their women and children squatted like animals along the rim of the smoking pit, stirring sagamité in their kettles. And Laforgue, coming toward this scene, felt his heart fill with an inexpressible relief. It was as though, walking a long and lonely road, he had come over a hill to the sight of a village, the village where he was born.

▼

That night he awoke with a start. Someone had kicked him in the back. Squirming around among the packed, stinking bodies of his companions, he saw the sorcerer Mestigoit, asleep, curled up like a hedgehog behind him. In the smoking firelight he saw Daniel lying near the door. At once, the thought came to him that, if today he had been lost forever in the woods, Daniel would have continued in a state of mortal sin and might die here among the Savages without benefit of confession. I cannot go on this way, Laforgue told himself. I must confront him. If he tries to go out tonight I must prevent him. Where is the girl?

But he could not see the girl. He crawled closer to Daniel. Dogs yelped and children cried and occasionally he heard furtive sounds which led him to believe that some of the Savages were copulating. He tried to pray. Gradually the sounds of crying children were replaced by an orchestra of grunts and snores. Again, he looked at the place where Daniel lay. He saw Daniel's back but then, with a start, realized that he had been mistaken. At once, he tried to sit up but found that the hunchback had rolled so close that he lay on the fold of his cassock. Carefully he disengaged himself, but as he did the sor-

cerer opened his glittering eyes and watched him with a
minatory stare.

Laforgue moved away, then lay down, feigning
sleep. After a few minutes, with great caution, he
crawled toward the doorway. When he rose up in the
night outside, his heart beat fast. Where are they? If I
find them I must not look at them but must call Daniel's
name at once. He stared about him, but all he saw was
the meadow's emptiness. He went down to the trees at
the edge of the meadow and walked along the rim of the
forest, calling softly, "Daniel? Daniel?" If Daniel heard,
would he answer or would he hide from sight? Laforgue
shivered. As he did, he thought he heard a sound, as
though someone were in pain. It came from the other
end of the meadow, in the direction of the river. Yes, it
came from the river. He ran across the meadow, running
toward the sound.

▼

She saw the sorcerer curl up behind the Blackrobe. Her
father said that the sorcerer would not let the Blackrobe
out of his sight until he found the answer. Yet this afternoon the Blackrobe had escaped the sorcerer and, in the
forest, had cast a spell on the hunting. That was what
Neehatin told the senior men. She was not supposed to
listen to such things. Unmarried women and those who
were married and had no children were themselves
treated as children. Yet she had risked creeping close to
the place where Neehatin held council, because she
feared for her lover. When Neehatin told the men that
the Blackrobe had cast a spell, he said that was why they

found no moose today in a place where the forest had promised moose.

When the sorcerer lay down beside the Blackrobe she saw that Iwanchou, her lover, was lying near the door. He had whispered to her that he would wait until the Blackrobe was asleep and then slip out to meet her in the trees. But tonight she feared the forest. The forest would be angry because the Blackrobe had cast a spell on it. Iwanchou was of the Blackrobe's tribe. The forest might revenge itself on him—and on her, if she were with him. But it grieved her that she would not meet him in the forest tonight. She wanted to fuck with him. Every night, she wanted to fuck with him. She did not understand what had happened. She had fucked with other boys and men. Everyone liked to do it, just as everyone liked to eat. The trick was to fuck before marriage and not have children. That was happiness, and she had been happy. But since thirty nights ago when she had first fucked with Iwanchou up at the eel fishery, she wanted only him. And he wanted only her. He became angry if she went with others. She remembered his anger that day on the riverbank when the Norman trader, who had fucked her before, caught hold of her, drunk, and fucked her again. Iwanchou would have killed the trader if the Blackrobe had not been there. Iwanchou was a strange boy. He feared the Blackrobe and did not want the Blackrobe to know that he and she fucked together. The Blackrobes did not fuck at all. Her father, Chomina, said that was because they were sorcerers. But that did not make sense to her. For sorcerers fucked. Even Mestigoit, who was as ugly as a porcupine and claimed to be a demon, had today shown the girls a stiff prick and begged them to let him do it.

When she asked Iwanchou why he feared to let the Blackrobe see him fuck, he said it was because of his god, who was also the Blackrobe's god. He said his god would be angry with him. Why would he be angry, she asked. What is wrong with fucking? Or is it because, as my father says, you Normans have no women of your own? Of course we have women, he said. In our country across the water there are many women. But she wondered if he lied. She remembered that he once said he had never fucked with a woman until he came to the Algonkin.

Now as she lay in the habitation and thought of these things, her eyes burned with tears which were not just tears of the smoke. She wanted to get up and go out with Iwanchou. She did not understand why, now, she wanted only him. Girls her age fucked with many men and received many presents before they married. It was the time of joy. After marriage, women were slaves. She had said all this to Iwanchou. She knew that he, too, had fucked with others, with Oonta and her young sister up at the eel fishery. But that was before I met you, he said. From now on we fuck only with each other. If it is presents you want, I will give you presents you cannot dream of. I will take you to my country, where you will eat every day as much as you want. She did not believe him. There was no place anywhere where one ate every day. She asked her father about that. Her father said it could be true that the Normans ate every day, but that was only because they were greedy pigs who would not share their food with others. They hide it in their habitations and refuse to pass it out when asked, her father said. No one should ever trust them, he said. They told the Hurons that if they embraced their god he would protect them from all harm. But that is shit, her father said. The Hurons who accept the Norman god die and starve like other people. And they practice a water sorcery, her father said. They put drops of water on the heads of sick people and babies, and the people and babies die. When she heard her father say these things she felt afraid. She asked Iwanchou if he would make her serve his god. But he said, "I no longer serve him myself. I serve the manitou."

The manitou was the great demon. Her father said the other Normans, the ones who came for furs, were madmen, bewitched by the manitou. They would give knives, wampum, kettles, awls, clothing, even muskets for the furs of beaver, otter, lynx and wildcat. They did not make ceremonial robes of these furs, as the people did, but instead took them out to their wooden islands in the river. When the snows came the islands disappeared into the wide water beyond and came back empty, many, many nights later when the winters were gone.

"Do not say that you serve the manitou," she told Iwanchou. "If you do, I must run away from you."

"Then we will run away together," he said. He wept when he said that. He said he did not have a plan for them. But they would be together always, he said.

"Why do you say that?" she asked him. "You know very well that when we reach the upper rapids, you and the Blackrobe will journey on to the Huron country, while we will stay here for the winter hunting. You will leave and I will never see you again."

"I won't leave you," Iwanchou said. "I will leave the Blackrobe when we reach the upper rapids. I will ask your father, Chomina, if I can become your husband and live and hunt with the Algonkin. I can teach them how to use their muskets," he said. "And I can get them more powder and shot, when the Blackrobes pay me what is owed me."

Sometimes, when he spoke like this, she remembered that although he was her age he was still a child. Her father would shit on him as a husband. Her father would say, "How can I give you as wife to a Norman? Everyone knows they are stupid as a blind elk. They do not know that this world is alive, that the trees speak, that the animals and fish are possessed of reason and will revenge themselves on us if we do not respect their dead. These stupid Normans feed the bones of beaver to dogs. The beaver does not forgive them," her father would say. "How could you take as husband a hunter the animals will not respect? You will starve."

When she told Iwanchou that he was wrong, that her father would never accept him as her husband, he said; "Then we will run away. Together."

"Why do you keep saying that?" she asked him. "It makes no sense. Where would we run?"

"I will take you to Québec," he said. "I will take you to Agnonha and ask that I be sent back with you to my country."

"In a wooden island?" she said. "No, no, I would be afraid."

"You need not be afraid," he said. "They are just great canoes. And when we reach my country, I will give you presents you have never dreamed of."

But she did not want presents. She did not know what to do. She wanted Iwanchou but she knew that soon, if the sorcerer said so, Iwanchou and the Blackrobe might die. She wept. She did not sleep. As the fire guttered into ashes, she felt Iwanchou tug at her robe. "Come," he said. And she went, crawling out into the cold, looking to see if the sky was angry. Iwanchou took her hand and led her toward the forest. "No," she said. "Not there."

"Why not?"

"The Blackrobe cast a spell on the forest. We must not go there."

Iwanchou smiled in the moonlight. "Who said that?"

"Mestigoit."

"That is shit," Iwanchou said. "Come."

"We will go to the river," she said. "Nicanis did not cast a spell upon the river." She pulled him around and began to run across the meadow, going down to the riverbank. He ran after her in the moonlight. He was laughing. When he was with her at night, he often laughed. During the day she had forbidden him to look at her or come near her. It was the custom for a young man, when he desired a girl as his betrothed one, not to look at her or speak to her or stay near her. She thought of him as her betrothed but did not want to tell him so. Instead she told him that he must stay away because she feared her father's anger. As he, for his part, feared the Blackrobe's anger. And so he did his best not to look on her while others were in view. He did not come near her except at night. But when they did meet, as now in the moonlight, he could not hide his joy. He laughed in happiness as, hand in hand, they went down the riverbank. They found a bed of ferns, well away from the habitation, and he lay on it, opened his breeches and showed her a stiff prick. "I am hungry," he said. "All night I was thinking of food. I asked myself, How can your people go so long without food? And then I thought of you. I had the answer. I no longer thought of food, I thought of you. Look," he said, "see what you have done. Kiss it." She knelt in front of him and kissed it. She shivered in the cold night air, but she was hot under her tunic. He pulled up her tunic and his tongue touched her breasts. She felt her nipples stiffen. She wanted to fuck now but she must ask him about the spell. "Why would Nicanis cast a spell so that we cannot find moose?"

"Shut up," he said. "Kiss me."

"Why would he want us to starve?" she said. "Answer me."

"How can I answer when you talk shit?" he said. "Come on. Lie down."

The bed of ferns was damp but, excited, she stripped off her tunic and her skirt and was naked for him, her only adornment a long necklace of white and purple beads made from the insides of shells. It hung and shook between her breasts as she reared over him and took his prick in her mouth, sucking it. Beneath her, he began to pull off his clothes so that he, too, would be naked. His skin was different from the skin of the people. She called it ghost skin and now, as she looked up along the white column of his belly and chest, it glistened silver in the night. He began to moan loudly and took her head in his hands, pulling her off his prick because he did not want to spend yet. She knelt and was about to turn and present her rear to him when she heard a sound of feet. Enemy? Quickly, she scrambled aside and threw his breeches over to Iwanchou, warning him to silence. As he dressed, the sound was louder; someone was running in their direction. She peered over the top of the ferns and saw the runner, his long skirts hiked up.

She whispered, "Nicanis!"

Iwanchou crouched down at once in the ferns, but she knew that was useless. The Blackrobe was coming their way; there was no place to hide. And then he appeared at the top of the riverbank and, looking down, discovered them. She heard him speak in the Norman tongue, his voice not angry, as she expected, but pleading and afraid. She saw the Blackrobe go to Iwanchou and try to embrace him. But Iwanchou pushed him away and came to her, helping her to fasten her tunic, his voice angry, speaking the strange Norman sounds. And then she saw the Blackrobe go down on his knees and put his hands together, palms flat against each other. The Blackrobe looked up at the sky and began to chant in the Norman speech.

It came upon her that the Blackrobe was putting a spell on them, because Blackrobes did not fuck and did not want others to fuck. And she said to Iwanchou, "Why do you let him do this? He is making a spell against us."

Iwanchou cradled her head against his chest. "No," he said. "He is speaking to his god. Come. Let us go back inside. I must think. We will have to decide."

"Decide what?" she asked him, but he did not answer. As they turned away from the kneeling Blackrobe, he stopped chanting and called out Iwanchou's Norman name, "Dan-Ya? Dan-Ya?" She saw that there were tears in the Blackrobe's eyes. Why did he weep? She looked at the sky but felt no danger. Night was the time of the dead. In the forest all around them, the dead walked and talked and watched what was happening here. What did the dead think of what they saw now, the Blackrobe, kneeling, casting some spell while she and Iwanchou walked away?

Or was it a spell? Did he, indeed, talk to his god, as Iwanchou said he did? And what did he say to him? And then her breath caught again as she saw that it was not only the dead who watched. Mestigoit stood among the trees. On his face was a smile, a smile she feared. He beckoned to her and to Iwanchou, summoning them to come to him. She would have obeyed, but Iwanchou shook his head and held her close. The sorcerer stepped out from the shelter of the trees and came up to her with his strange dancing step, a man small as a child, his back bunched like an eagle's wings. "You have joined the dead, Annuka," he said to her. "See?" He pointed to the kneeling figure of the Blackrobe. "He has cast the spell of death on you."

"Come away," Iwanchou said to her.

"Where will you go?" the hunchback said, and laughed. "Where will you go?"

▼

When he saw the girl naked below him on the riverbank, Laforgue averted his eyes. He heard a scuffling sound. When he looked again, Daniel was shielding her as she dressed. "Daniel," Laforgue said. Words would not come. He bent his head.

"Go away, Father," Daniel said. "Go away."

"I cannot." He moved toward the boy, as if to embrace him. "Daniel, let us pray together, for your sin and for mine."

But Daniel pushed him away. "Leave me alone," he said, in a choked, angry voice. "I don't want to pray. I am going to live with this girl."

"No. If you do, your sin will be my sin for all eternity. Listen to me. God will forgive you, as He will forgive us all, if only we ask His forgiveness. Daniel, kneel with me."

And making the sign of the cross, Laforgue went down on his knees in the grass, joining his hands in prayer. "Merciful God, our Savior, we implore Your pardon—"

But as he said the words, the girl spoke loudly in the Savage tongue. "Why do you let him do this? He is making a spell against us."

He heard Daniel say something about him praying to his god. Then, pulling her after him, the boy scrambled up the riverbank. "Daniel?" Laforgue called. "Daniel?" as they fled across the meadow. He stood up and saw them at the rim of the trees, then saw the sorcerer appear. The sorcerer said something Laforgue could not hear. The girl turned and ran away. Laforgue watched Daniel run after her, catch up with her and embrace her. Embracing, they went toward the habitation. I will wait until morning, he told himself. I will wait until morning and then I will speak to him, alone. What does he mean, he is going to live with her? The devil has addled him as he addled me.

He stood, looking down the meadow. The sorcerer was coming his way. In his left hand the sorcerer held

his flat drum, and as he crossed the meadow he began to
shake it. He came closer, beginning his shuffling dance.
The sound of the drum's pebbles rattled like hailstones
in the chamber of Laforgue's infected ear. In the moonlight he saw the sorcerer's glittering eyes.

"Demon," cried the sorcerer. "Are you there? Are
you still hiding in the Blackrobe? Answer me."

"Be quiet," Laforgue said. "The others are asleep.
There is no demon."

"No!" Shaking his drum, the sorcerer began his
horrible howls.

"Stop it!" Laforgue shouted, and to his surprise the
sorcerer stopped, his movements arrested as though Laforgue had plunged a javelin into his chest.

"Come then," the sorcerer said quietly. "Come, Nicanis. I will show you something."

Beckoning to Laforgue in his usual theatrical manner, the sorcerer led him to the edge of the trees. "Listen," the sorcerer said. "What do you hear?"

Laforgue heard nothing except the crackling of
small branches and the night sighing of swaying boughs.

"Well?" asked the sorcerer.

"I hear nothing. My ears are poor."

"Do you not hear Her voice?"

"What voice? I tell you my ears are poor."

"Look, then. Look over there." The sorcerer
pointed, almost timidly, at a dark huddle of trees. "See?
She wears a robe of beautiful hair. It is the hair of the
men She has killed. Just now, when you were down by
the river, I heard Her call your name. 'Nicanis?' She
called. "I knew then that the demon had left you. Look,
now. Can you not see Her?"

"I see nothing," Laforgue said.

"Then come away," the sorcerer said. "Let us go together to the habitation."

Unwillingly, Laforgue followed the hunchback across the moonlit meadow. He felt numbed with the cold. He saw that the sorcerer kept glancing back at the trees.

"Ah," said the sorcerer. "She is gone. But She will be back."

"Who are you speaking of?" Laforgue said.

The sorcerer smiled. "How strange you Normans are. You are deaf and blind as are the dead in daytime. You say you know many things, and yet you speak like small children with few words and no understanding. She called your name. If you were one of us your heart would burst with terror. Yet you hear nothing, you feel nothing."

"Who is this 'she'?" Laforgue asked. "Is it some sorcery, some devil you fear?"

The sorcerer smiled. "I told you, you are as a child; you see nothing, you hear nothing, you know nothing. Poor Nicanis." He held aside the flap of skin at the doorway. "Come. Let us sleep. Even I cannot help you now."

5

Next morning it snowed. When the Savages emerged from their habitation, a thick fall had weighted the branches of the surrounding forest, whitened and concealed the ground of the meadow and filled the air in a blinding mist. The Savages seemed pleased. Children hurled themselves into this first real snow of winter, rolling like little logs down the slopes of the riverbank. Dogs yelped excitedly and ran about, pissing yellow streams in the white carpet. The women began to tear down the walls of the night's habitation, rolling the bark up and hurrying to pack it in the canoes. Laforgue, seeking Daniel, came upon him as he covered his musket in a deerskin cloth.

"Good morning."

The boy looked at him, his eyes cold. Snow covered his shoulders like a cloak. "There is no time to talk now, Father. We must start at once. Neehatin wants to reach the Isle of Dyes by early afternoon. That means hard paddling."

"Very well," Laforgue said. "We won't speak about last night. But what is this talk of leaving to live with that girl? Father Jerome's life may depend on our reaching Ihonatiria before winter sets in. Without you, I cannot do it."

"We're talking about today, not the future," the boy said. "Come. It's important that we hurry."

Laforgue felt his face flush with anger. "What is more important than your immortal soul?"

"Hurry!" the boy said again.

"Answer me. What could you do now that would be more important than going down on your knees and asking God's forgiveness?"

But as he spoke, the boy turned away and ran toward the canoes.

"Daniel, listen to me."

"You listen to *me*," the boy called back. "If you care about the life of Father Jerome, get in the canoe. Hurry. They do not like to be kept waiting."

"Don't be impertinent." Laforgue's voice rose in anger. "No matter what you think of me, I am a priest. There is a respect you owe my cloth." But as he said this he felt, suddenly, the foolishness of his words. What respect? What sort of priest was he? Why did he speak to this boy as to a pupil in a schoolroom when he knew, and the boy knew, that they were alone, abandoned here in this land God gave to Cain, the devil's land, living among barbarians who now impatiently pushed their canoes out into the stream?

He ran down to his canoe, throwing in his cloak, pulling off his clogs to wade in the icy water, scrambling over the side of the fragile craft as the Algonkian paddlers watched. The canoes, forming a long snake, moved swiftly out into the great river. Snow blinded Laforgue as he removed his wide-brimmed hat so as not to impede the vision of the paddler behind him. Two dogs clambered over him to nestle in the pile of belongings in the center of the canoe.

When he took up the paddle and began to stroke, his head felt faint and his ears rang with the familiar deafening noise he had come to fear. He stared ahead into the blinding mist of snow; the chill air formed tiny icicles in the hair of his beard and eyebrows. Someone kicked him from behind, almost unbalancing him in the narrow canoe. He turned, slewing to one side, to let the child who had kicked him pass by and scramble up with the other children on the snow-covered pile of baggage. But as this child settled itself, it turned and looked back at him. Through the veil of snowflakes he saw the wizened face and glittering eyes of the sorcerer, Mestigoit.

▼

All morning the canoes moved upriver. The storm did not abate. At times the wind seemed to shift and the snow beat upon their backs instead of their faces. On either side, the forest, mantled by snow, seemed to blur and disappear into the white woolen cloud of sky, as though the land itself had melted into the desolation of winter. Laforgue, paddling, felt his arms and shoulders ache as though he had been flayed. His knees and thighs froze in their cramped position, and numbness spread down his left leg, often causing him to half topple at the end of his stroke. Try as he might, he could not keep pace with the Savage ahead of him, and there were times when he was forced to let his paddle trail in the water and, panting, dizzy, bow his head, his ears ringing, his body racked with pain.

Early in the afternoon he saw, mistily, in the distance, the shores of a large island in the center of the river, and as he did, the snake of canoes turned left, going toward a landing place. The Island of Dyes, Daniel had called this place, and Laforgue remembered reading in Father Brabant's account of his journey that this was where the Algonkin found a red root with which they dyed their ceremonial robes. The island was heavily wooded. Laforgue, his clogs tied around his neck, his cassock hiked up, scrambled about in the shallows, helping pull his canoe clear of the water, pushing it up onto the snow-covered shore.

The Savages, on landing, at once tied to their feet the large flat disks made of thongs and wood which the French called *raquettes*. Laforgue, undoing his bundle of belongings, took out these snowshoes on which, at Québec, he had spent many hours of practice. Having tied them on, he maneuvered carefully across the snow, but now, in real winter snow, his practice did not stand him in good stead. Reaching a deep drift, he toppled into it. Gleeful children ran around him and one of the Algonkian men helped him right himself, laughing, saying,

"Stand up, you silly prick. Have you been drinking the Norman drink that makes you fall down?"

"Thank you," Laforgue said, and smiled. One must always smile and give thanks and never lose one's temper, for the Savages were slow to anger and surprisingly good-humored about their own trials and sufferings.

"Lift your feet up like this, Nicanis," the man said, and demonstrated. Slowly, Laforgue went up the incline. Beside him, adept on a child's set of snowshoes, the hunchback moved with a light, hopping step.

At the top of the incline stood Neehatin and Chomina, both armed for a hunt. "Today you will come with us when we seek moose," the hunchback said. "Neehatin has told me to watch you, Blackrobe. No spells against the hunt, do you hear? Pray to your god. Ask him to send us moose."

"I will do that," Laforgue said. He saw that Neehatin was looking down at him. The Algonkian leader's face made him think of the stone image of a dead Saxon king he had seen carved on a tomb in Bayeux. Neehatin raised his arm and shouted some orders of which Laforgue heard only "Beyond the trees . . . Chomina with five men . . . Ougebemat, the ravine . . ." and then, "Iwanchou, put away your musket and take a javelin. We do not want the noise of your cannon."

"Come," the hunchback said. "Follow me. Lift your feet like this."

And so, moving among sparse trees, plodding on the wide, flat snowshoes, Laforgue followed the hunters into the white unknown. A chill wind caused powdered snow to blow off the tops of drifts in a fine, sugary mist. Laforgue, keeping as close as he could to the hunchback's pace, gradually became aware that the others had gone on ahead and were lost to his sight. Through the trees they came out onto a long snow-covered hillside which stretched down for half a mile to end in a wooded ravine. At the top of this slope, he again saw the hunters. They had cut and fashioned long poles, to which they attached javelins tipped by stone points. Balancing these poles, they went cautiously down the sloping hillside. The hunchback turned and put his filthy hand over Laforgue's mouth, warning him to silence.

The hunters spread out in a wide, wavering line, becoming smaller until their figures were like children's, far down the white slopes. Suddenly, the hunchback tensed and pointed. From a clump of trees, ungainly, floundering in the deep snow, came a male and two female moose. Their long thin legs plunged into the drifts and they staggered, mired as though the snow were a white glue. The hunters, seeing them, advanced, not running but stalking them as though afraid to come too close. Laforgue saw Chomina turn and give a signal to the others. All stopped.

Chomina was closest to the animals. Raising his unwieldy javelin he hurled it, striking a moose in the neck. The animal reared up in the deep snow. The remaining two, frantic, began a slow muddy gallop back toward the trees. At once, other hunters, some hurling their javelins, some jabbing with them like spears, circled and attacked the injured moose. Laforgue saw the animal fall, saw the snow stained by blood. Five hunters now burst from another part of the forest, trying to block off the escape of the two fleeing animals. The javelins flew. One of the moose tripped and fell, and the hunters, swift, sure, incredibly agile on their flat snowshoes, closed in for the kill. The unharmed moose, a doe, had reached higher ground where the snows were not deep and now, at speed, fled to safety along the tree line. At that, the hunters broke their silence with howls of triumph. Two of the large animals lay dead in the snow. The hunchback turned to Laforgue, his glittering eyes filled with joy. "Ho, ho," he cried, uttering the guttural Savage cry of pleasure. "Your god has answered you, Nicanis. Those moose have died for you. I told you the demon had gone out from under your black robe, you lucky old prick. Now, we will eat. Yes, tonight we will truly eat."

But Laforgue was looking about for Daniel. At last he saw the boy standing close to the first-killed moose, as the Algonkin began with their knives to hack the animal into sections. From the area where the canoes were beached, women appeared, pulling behind them the long strips of bark with which they enclosed their habitation. The women went down to the scene of carnage and the hunters loaded pieces of the dismembered animal onto these makeshift sleds. Daniel was helping to skin the hind leg of a moose, and as Laforgue watched the boy, his hands and forearms stained with blood, his long hair flowing down his back, his clothing greasy, he seemed, at a distance, indistinguishable from the young men around him. And again Laforgue thought of other Frenchmen he had seen in this wild and empty land: of the fur trader Mercier, half naked, eating at the kettles; of the young coureurs de bois who went into the woods with the Algonkin in search of furs and came back to Québec, wild, corrupted, sleeping with the Savage girls. How was it that, in a few months of living like animals among these barbarians, they could forget the civilization they had left behind and, with no fear of eternal damnation, embrace the ways of ignorance and filth in which these barbarians lived? Is Belial more beautiful than Jesus? Laforgue asked himself. Impossible. Then how can it be that he is more ardently loved, more promptly obeyed and more devotedly adored?

But now he was given little time to reflect on such matters. For all around him, as though in drunken euphoria, the Savages were bustling about, calling out foul slanders on each other, laughing and cavorting like buffoons as they dragged their catch back to the encampment where the fires were already ablaze in the snow. The kettles were slung and the meat was thrown in. Children and dogs romped in the snowdrifts while the hunters, as though to celebrate their victory, began to gamble among each other, tossing stones in a bowl as they waited for the meat to cook. As the Jesuit warmed his freezing feet and tried to dry the hem of his robe at the flames, Neehatin approached him. The sorcerer, who had been trying to caress a girl little older than a child, stopped his depredations and at once came over, as though to eavesdrop.

"Well, Nicanis," Neehatin said, smiling. "Mestigoit tells me he has pulled that demon out of your asshole. Is that right?"

"There was no demon," Laforgue said, remembering to smile. But he did not hear what Neehatin said next; his ears began their painful ringing. "What was that?" he asked.

"I said, can your god bring us food every day? Mestigoit thinks you can cast a spell on game. Can you cast a good spell tomorrow as you did today? I mean, bring us beavers as well as moose?"

"I can ask," Laforgue said. "But I do not know if my God will think us worthy of his blessings."

"Nicanis is a cunning old prick, isn't he?" Mestigoit said, prancing around in his usual irritating fashion. "He's not going to tell us anything, is he?"

"Just tell us where to get more moose," Neehatin said, laughing. "If you can do that, we'll follow you anywhere you want to go. Even past the Great Rapids. That's a promise, Nicanis. Talk to that god of yours, and if he brings me moose—oh, yes, and some beaver and a few fat birds as well—then I promise you I'll kiss his fucking toes as you do."

"My God can do more than find food," Laforgue said, but as he spoke he saw that Neehatin was no longer listening. He had turned away and now called out something to the women around the fires. One of the women took a piece of meat from a kettle, put it on a bark plate and brought it to the Algonkian leader. At once, he tore off a small strip and handed the remainder of the plate to Laforgue. He held up the strip of meat which he had torn off and said, "This is for your Hesu. Is that his name?"

"Jesus is his name," Laforgue said.

"Hee-sus. All right. Heesus, I give you this piece of moose and ask you for more." He threw the piece of meat into the fire, where it roasted and then shriveled in the flames. "Now, eat," he said, turning to Laforgue. "We will all eat our fucking faces full. Right?"

At that a great roar of joy went up from the men, women and children assembled around the kettles, and at once the women began ladling out pieces to all comers who proffered their empty bark plates. As Laforgue sat down beside the flames to consume his portion, dogs, frantic with hunger, barked and pushed at him, one sticking its snout right into the plate, upsetting the meat onto the snow. Hastily, Laforgue retrieved it. After ten days of eating only the foul-tasting sagamité, this half-cooked meat now seemed to him as fine as any beef he had eaten in Normandy. Famished, he wolfed it down and, following the example of the others, got up and went to the kettles for more. All around him were smiling faces and a noise of shouting, laughter, foul banter. Again, he was impressed by the way in which the Savages, although they must be as famished as he, did not jostle each other and seek out more than their share. Indeed, as he approached the kettles, the man in front of him turned and dumped on his plate the piece of meat he had pulled out for himself. Laforgue moved on into a throng of Savages, eating from his plate as he walked. He was searching for Daniel. Now is the time to speak with him; now, when all are occupied and before we lie down for the night. But as he walked, his ears began to ring. The heavy toll of the day's paddling, the freezing cold and the pain from the old injury to his foot all conspired to make him shiver as though he ran a fever. He remembered that he had not said his nightly office, remembered that in these moments of feasting he had thought of nothing but eating his fill. Why had he marveled just now that other men could become brutalized in these wilds? Was it any wonder that eating was the Savages' highest joy when, cast out from the sight of God, they dwelled here, in this harsh and unforgiving land, dependent as wild animals on finding prey? Would it ever be possible to convert such people? It is as though this country is far from the sun of God's warmth. Even I, who now beseech His aid, can only think of eating my fill, then brutishly huddling among other warm bodies in the smoking stench of tonight's habitation. My mind is fogged with pain and weariness. I can no longer think.

And then he saw Daniel, sitting among six or seven young hunters, licking his fingers as he finished gnawing on a bone. At once Laforgue went over and squatted down beside him. In the firelight the boy's features seemed to shine as though, like the Savages, he had greased his skin. He did not speak but resumed gnawing at the ragged fringe of meat which adhered to the bone.

"Why do you hide from me," Laforgue said. It was not a question, but an accusation.

Daniel stopped eating. He stared into the flames of the fire. "Because I am ashamed."

Laforgue felt his heart beat hard in his chest. If only he knew that I too have sinned, he might speak to me.

"I also am ashamed," Laforgue said. "I am ashamed for myself. Let him who is without sin cast the first stone. I can cast no stone."

"What are you talking about?" The boy kept looking into the fire. "You don't understand."

Laforgue bowed his head. "Daniel, I too have committed a sin of the flesh."

"You?" The boy turned to him for a moment, astonished. Then he laughed. "What sin did *you* commit, Father? Something you did long ago, in France?"

"No, no. A sin of intent. Here. With that girl."

Again the boy looked at him, a side glance, suspicious and confused. "My uncle does not like the Jesuits; he wanted me to go as an apprentice with the Récollet Fathers. The Jesuits lie for the greater glory of God, my uncle told me. The end justifies the means. One must never trust what they say."

"I am telling the truth."

"But why? To win me over, isn't that it?"

"We have sinned equally in the sight of God," Laforgue said. "Perhaps my sin is greater because I am a priest. Now we must ask His forgiveness and promise to amend our lives. I want you to kneel with me and say an act of contrition. And promise that we will avoid further temptation."

"Amen," the boy said sarcastically. "Father, don't you know that life isn't so simple for the rest of us? We are not Jesuits. God has not chosen us to be His special servants."

"God chose you to come with me," Laforgue said. "And now, Daniel—Daniel, listen to me. I am afraid. I am afraid of this country. I am afraid of this mission. I am afraid of what is happening here. I don't mean the ordinary dangers: starvation, capture, death. I mean the other, the greater danger. Perhaps it is heresy to say it, but in the last few days, as we go on, I know more and more that the devil rules this land. Belial rules here; he rules the hearts and minds of these poor people. Through them he seeks to wound Our Savior. Through them, and through our weakness. Through that girl, for instance."

"Woman is the devil's instrument, the fount of pollution," the boy said, chanting it mockingly. "Please, Father, I've heard it all before."

"That does not mean it is not true."

"It can be true or not true, it doesn't matter. I said I am ashamed. Do you know why? Because I have failed God, and because it means nothing to me."

"How can it mean nothing, since you feel ashamed?"

"Stop it," the boy said, in an angry whisper. "Don't try to trick me with a Jesuit's arguments. I am not going to give up this life, do you hear?"

"You are not going to give up that girl, you mean. What life are you talking about? This life—living like an animal?"

"Animals? The Savages are truer Christians than we will ever be. They have no ambitions. They think we are mean and foolish because we love possessions more than they do. They live for each other, they share everything, they do not become angry with each other, they forgive each other things which we French would never forgive."

"I know all that," Laforgue said. "I know it, and it fills me with shame. Their patience is extraordinary."

"It is more than patience. You do not know them as I do. Annuka tells me about the mysteries of this land and these forests. It is there that they find their spiritual strength. They think us blind and stupid. They say we are less intelligent than they are, because we ignore these mysteries."

"What mysteries?" Laforgue said. His ears rang. He had to strain to hear what the boy was saying.

"The mysteries of this world. They believe that all things have a soul: men, animals, fish, forests, rivers."

"That is because Belial rules here," Laforgue said.

"The devil infects their minds, making them resist the truth of our teachings."

"What teachings?" the boy said. "Why should they believe in your world after death when they already have an afterworld of their own?"

"What are you talking about? They do not believe in an afterworld. Father Brabant, who studied them for years, says they have no concept of an afterlife."

"He's wrong."

"So you know more than Father Brabant?"

"Yes, because they would never trust him. To them he is a Blackrobe, and all Blackrobes are sorcerers. They would not tell him of their world of the dead."

Laforgue stared at the angry young face in the firelight. Around them, the feasting Savages had begun to sing their monotonous chants of celebration. "What world?" Laforgue said.

"The world of the dead."

"And where is this world?"

"They believe that at night the dead see. They move about, animals and men, in the forests of night. The souls of men hunt the souls of animals, moving through forests made up of the souls of trees which have died."

"Is that what she told you?" Laforgue smiled. "But what childish reasoning! Do they believe that these dead souls eat and drink, as we do?"

The boy looked at him with scorn. "Is that harder to believe in than a paradise where we all sit on clouds and look at God? Or burn forever in the flames of hell?"

Laforgue felt his anger rise. He clenched his hands together. "So they have a world of the dead, a world of night when the dead come alive. And what do they do in the daytime, these dead things?"

"She said, in the daytime they are blind. The dead Savages sit like this, she said." Daniel crouched on the ground and put his elbows on his knees, his head between his hands, mimicking the posture which Laforgue had seen the Algonkin adopt when a sickness came upon them. "When night comes, they rise up," the boy said. "They go to the chase."

Laforgue shivered as with a fever. He felt cold sweat trickle down the back of his neck as the boy, squatting there like a Savage, repeated to him the foolish fantasies of these barbarians. "Forgive me," Laforgue said. "But do you realize what you are saying?"

"I am telling you what *they* believe. I did not say that I believe it. I am telling you that you will never truly convert them to your teachings."

"You wish to distract me," Laforgue said. "As the Evil One has distracted you and filled you with a lust, so strong that it drives out the fear you should feel now. The fear of losing your immortal soul."

"Why do I talk to you?" The boy jumped up and stood over Laforgue as though he would strike him.

"If you die tonight, in your state of mortal sin, you will find out that there *is* a hell," Laforgue said. "A hell for all eternity."

"Good night, Father," the boy said and, turning, went along the edge of the pit of smoking kettles, mingling with the crowd of jostling, chanting, feasting Savages. Laforgue did not follow him. Instead, his shivering increased until his whole body shook as if in a fever. His limbs ached and his stomach, sated with half-cooked food, became queasy, making him feel he would vomit. He rocked to and fro by the fire, staring at the flames, his mind confusedly remembering what had been discussed. If I become ill and unable to travel, the Savages will show me no kindness. Even to their own, when sick, they pretend indifference. Father Bourque warned that if I become ill I must conceal it from them. I must be strong. I should pray.

Shutting his eyes, he willed his weary mind to prayer but, instead, fell into a doze. He started, catching himself, as he almost tumbled headlong in the snow. All he could think of now was the time when, their feasting over, the Savages would crawl into their habitation and he could at last, amid warm bodies, find surcease from his fever and pain in long weary sleep. Tomorrow he must rise and paddle with the others. Tomorrow, they would journey on.

▼

Neehatin woke. He stretched out his arm to the pouch in which, before sleeping, he had placed some scraps of meat, as was the custom after a feast. He looked at the rooftop opening of the habitation and knew that the sun had climbed the first wall of sky. He ate slowly, chewing the meat and spitting out gristle. Then he crawled past the huddled bodies of others and left the habitation. Some were already up. He saw the Blackrobe kneeling by the river, washing his neck and face. Chomina and Amantacha and Ougebemat were cutting hunting poles as he had told them to last night. He went to them.

"We will go down through the ravine to look for

tracks," he said. "Then we will move to the high slopes. Are you ready for that, you silly cows?"

"You find us moose and we'll climb twenty fucking slopes," Amantacha said.

"Neehatin," said Ougebemat, "we have been talking. Tell me. Do you think the Blackrobe's spell brought moose to this island? Last winter and the winter before there were no moose here."

"There is a causeway on the far shore," Neehatin said. "At the end of summer, the water level is low there. A family of stupid moose might wander over here and then, when the water rose, find themselves blocked. No way back."

"What a wonderful fucking mind this man has," Ougebemat said, and all laughed good-naturedly. But they knew his explanation was the right one. And they prefer my explanation, Neehatin thought. They don't want to think they are eating moose brought here by the spell of a Norman sorcerer.

"So when do we start?" Chomina asked. Chomina looked at Neehatin with respect but no love.

"We'll start now," Neehatin said. "Better send the children on ahead to camp on the other side of the island. The women can follow them with the heavy bundles and kettles. We'll beach the canoes here."

"Have you told that fart of a Blackrobe?" Chomina asked. "He's going to shit himself."

"Fuck the Blackrobe," Neehatin said. "Leave him to me."

"If the children start now, they should reach camp well before dark," Ougebemat said. "It is only a half day's journey, even for the little ones."

"Give them some stuff to carry," Neehatin said. "Let the little fuckers get used to it." The others laughed. They loved their children, but he was right. They must be taught to carry.

"What about the Normans?" Chomina said.

"They come with us. I want to keep those cows in front of me, not behind me."

Neehatin left, then, and went down to the river. "Nicanis?" he called. The Blackrobe came to him, smiling, nodding his head as the Normans always did when they met you after the night's sleeping. The Blackrobe looked sick.

"Are you all right?" Neehatin asked. "You look as if you had shit yourself." He laughed and the Blackrobe laughed, but as always it was forced. He laughed as though his teeth hurt.

"Yes, I am well," the Blackrobe said. "It was good to eat that meat last night."

"And we'll find more today," Neehatin said. "There must be five moose in that family. We've only killed two. Now we'll go after the others."

"But surely we should go on," the Blackrobe said. "The snows have started. I am very worried. We must go on today."

"No, Nicanis. First we will kill moose and eat moose, and what we do not eat we will smoke and take with us. Then we will travel fast for many days."

The Blackrobe hesitated. Neehatin saw the sweat of a sick man on his brow. "Neehatin, my friend," the Blackrobe said, speaking, as always, like a little child who has just learned his first words. "If you must hunt today, I will stay here and rest."

"Fuck that," Neehatin said, laughing. "We're going to camp on the far slopes tonight. You're coming."

"But couldn't I stay here and wait for your return?"

Neehatin looked up at the sky. The sky gave no sign. Why did this sorcerer want to stay behind? Was there some danger he knew would overtake them? "No," Neehatin said. "I'll tell you what. Since you're so fucking tired, you won't have to carry a burden today. Mestigoit will be with you, and you'll come with us, with the hunters. Get your shoes on. I must go."

He did not wait for the Blackrobe to do any more complaining. The Normans always complained. They gave you good presents but then reminded you that they had given them. They worried about everything just like old women. They were full of shit. Neehatin went up the riverbank, calling, "Women with children, women with children."

Families were coming out of the habitation. He looked back at the river. The river went its way. It said nothing of danger ahead.

"Give them burdens," he said to the mothers. "Not too heavy. Make little sleds and have them drag them after themselves as you do. Start now. We will follow later. We are going to find moose."

He heard the sorcerer's chuckling laugh and turned to find the little man at his heels. "Did I hear you say moose?" the sorcerer said.

"Yes, moose. There must be at least three of them over on the farther slopes. I want you to travel in our rear. We will take Iwanchou with Chomina's men, but you will stay close to the Blackrobe. We are going to move fast, and that cow cannot use his shoes. If you see him start a sorcery, leave him and come to tell me. He is sick with the shaking sickness. Did you know that?"

The sorcerer smiled. "Of course I know it. Two nights ago, in the forest, the She Manitou smiled on him. The flesh-eater."

Neehatin felt alarm. "You saw Her?"

"Yes."

"Then why are *you* not sick?"

"I am a demon," said the sorcerer. "She will not harm one of Her own."

"You're a great little fart," Neehatin said, laughing, although in truth he was always uneasy when he spoke with Mestigoit. It was true that Mestigoit was said to be a demon who had entered a woman and had been born through her cunt. Perhaps he lied about seeing the She. "Are you sure you saw Her?" he asked again.

The hunchback smiled, showing teeth pointed like a dog's. "I saw. She did not look at me. She looked at the Blackrobe."

"Well, fuck it," Neehatin said, trying to joke. "That makes it easy, doesn't it?"

"Easy?" The wizened face no longer smiled.

"If She eats him in a night or two, we will not have to go as far as the Great Rapids. We will have gained our presents from Agnonha for nothing."

"There are no presents given by the Normans which are not paid for," the sorcerer said.

"What the fuck are you talking about?" Neehatin said, still trying to make a joke of it.

"I mean what I mean and you know what I mean," the sorcerer said. "We are two nights from the beginning of danger. The Blackrobe may not die. He is a sorcerer, a Norman sorcerer. And they are hard to kill."

"Normans shit and eat and bleed and die just like other men," Neehatin said. "Want to bet on it? I have two beaver skins who say if the She looked on him, he will not last two nights."

"I have no beaver skins," the sorcerer said. "I have this knife."

"My knife against yours, then, you little prick."

And, at last, the sorcerer laughed.

▼

It had snowed again in the night. By the time the hunters reached the high ground on the far side of the ravine, the tracks of the moose which had escaped them yesterday were completely obliterated. But the snow was now deep, even on the high ground. Moose, which could run fast as deer on hard ground, were helpless in deep snow. Chomina took one slope, Neehatin the other. The moose could smell hunters from a great distance. As the Algonkin advanced, the moose would seek the shelter of trees to hide.

The hunters covered both slopes and then fanned out in a long line. The moose must have gone down to the far end of the island. The land narrowed there. The hunters moved their net all morning, walking on and on in their snowshoes over the deep soft snow. It was late afternoon when they saw tracks. The tracks were like long thin holes in the snow. The hunters stopped and smiled at each other. All were silent. The tracks led them toward a wooded place. Chomina moved his men into close formation as they approached the trees. Neehatin did likewise. Moving in a semicircle, the hunters entered the woods. The wooded place was not large. The hunters raised their long javelins and, silent, went through the dark spare aisles of trees. By now, the wind was in their faces. The wind was kind. The moose might not even scent them until they were close. But then, ahead, they saw a male and two female moose, blundering through the trees, plunging in panic, making for the open snow at the end of the woods.

The hunters began to run, swift on their unwieldy snowshoes. There was no longer a need for silence, so they began to yell in order to panic the moose. The moose blundered into the open, sinking to their bellies as their long thin legs plunged into the drifts. The hunters now closed the circle, moving closer their net of spears. Chomina saw that one of the females had turned and was now nearest to the Norman boy, Iwanchou. It was to Iwanchou that he gave the command to strike. The boy struck well, his javelin entering the moose's neck at a place where the blood ran thick. Within minutes, all three moose lay skewered; the male had plunged its antlers into a snowdrift. The hunters raised their javelins and shouted to each other. Chomina, seeing Iwanchou with the others, went up to him and put his arm around him. "You silly pale prick," he said, laughing. "I think your mother was Algonkin."

The boy laughed. "Maybe she was," he said. "That would make me stupid like you. But that's all right. I like to hunt and eat just like the rest of you. Maybe I'll become Algonkian myself."

Chomina looked at him. He knew this boy was fucking Annuka. He had seen the presents he gave her, necklaces and other goods. "Why would you become one of us?" Chomina asked. "When you work for the

Blackrobes in Québec, they say you eat every day. You build wooden habitations for them and you have no need to hunt."

"I like to hunt," the boy said. "I love you fuckers, don't you know that?"

"Better than the Blackrobes?"

"Yes."

"You're full of shit," Chomina said, laughing. "Come. Let's get these moose out of here."

▼

The sun was low on the horizon when Mestigoit and Laforgue, moving in the wake of the hunters, saw them ahead, dragging their slaughtered prey. The moose had been cut into sections and placed on narrow makeshift sleds of wooden runners covered by peeled strips of bark. The hunters, harnessed like pack animals by cords bound around their foreheads, dragged these heavy sleds through the deep snows. Laforgue, half delirious from fever, wondered how the hunters could move their legs under this heavy burden. His own snowshoes had become weighted with snow, and each time he stumbled in a drift, it seemed as if someone beneath the snow pulled on his ankles as though to wrench them from their sockets.

When, at last, their caravan came to the new campsite, the women had already arrived, lit the fires and cut the poles for the night's habitation. The children, weary from their long journey, sat uncharacteristically listless on their bundles but now rose and ran yelling toward the hunters and their prey. Because of the deep snow, the habitation must be built in the true winter manner, and so, laying aside their harness, the Algonkian men removed their snowshoes and, using them as shovels, began to clear a large circle in the snow, digging into it to a depth of three feet. Even the hunchback helped in this work for, as Laforgue was to discover, it would take three hours in the shivering cold to prepare this place where they would sleep. The pit dug by the Savages made a white wall like the wall of a small house, surrounding the sleeping place on all sides except where a break was made for an entrance. Some twenty poles, which the women had already cut and trimmed from the surrounding woods, were then planted in the snow to form the scaffolding of a roof, converging loosely at the top. The long strips of bark, sewn together, which formed the roof of the previous habitations were now placed over this frame. The floor and walls of the habitation were then lined with small branches of fir, and a skin was draped over the entrance. Only when this work was finished, at a time when the sky was already dark, did the Algonkin return to the fires and begin to cook the slaughtered moose.

Laforgue, shivering although he sat close to the flames, was astonished to see that the Savages who had worked for hours in the freezing snow pit sweated on their return as though the night were warm. Merriment and the usual insults began as the first pieces of meat were thrown into the kettles. Laforgue, who had been reading his office by the light of the fire, sat apart. His hands, icy in their mittens, stung as though he were a schoolboy who had been caned. Indeed, there seemed no part of his body which did not suffer its own particular torment. He sat alone. He did not look for Daniel, nor did the boy come near him. All around him he heard the Savages shouting their obscenities, the dogs barking, the chants of the lugubrious Savage songs of triumph and the rattling sounds of the sorcerer's drum.

"Nicanis."

He looked up. Above him, holding a bark plate filled with meat, was Neehatin. "Eat," said Neehatin, handing him the plate. He took it, but his hands, frozen and stiff in their mittens, let the plate spill, the meat falling on the ground. At once, two dogs came bounding over. Neehatin kicked them away.

"Are you sick, Nicanis?"

"My hands are cold."

"Let me see." The leader squatted down and slipped off Laforgue's mitten. He felt his hand. "Shit," he said. "They *are* cold. Here." From his tunic he took his own mittens and put them on Laforgue's hands. The mittens were warm from the heat of his body. "I will take yours," he said. He laughed. "Nicanis, let me give you some advice."

"Advice?"

"You must not travel with us in winter. We are going to kill you."

Neehatin was smiling, and so Laforgue felt he must smile too. "I am stronger than you think," he said.

"A sick man on a sled is heavy baggage," Neehatin said. "If he's going to die anyway, why drag him along? Better to put a hatchet in his head." He laughed uproariously, throwing back his head, showing his perfect teeth.

"I'd better not get sick, then."

"Eat your meat," Neehatin said. "Tomorrow we will smoke what is left of these moose; then we'll go back to the canoes and continue our journey." He walked off with no farewells. Laforgue looked at the meat and felt he would vomit. Carefully, making sure he was not seen, he wrapped it in a cloth and hid it in his belongings. Then, feeling as though he would faint, he got up, left the fires and went to the newly built habitation. When he crawled inside, the place was empty, save for two of the older women who tended the smoking fire. Laforgue lay down close to the fire, drawing his cloak around his shoulders. Although his face was seared by the heat of the flames, his back shivered from the cold of the snow-packed wall behind him. Huddled in a fetal crouch, he sought sleep.

▼

At dawn her mother tugged on her hair, waking her. Together, they crawled toward the door. The other women who had been chosen last night were already outside and starting the fires. When the fires were burning well, her mother went to call her father. He came with six men. They took the male moose which had not been eaten last night. They removed all the bones, as was the custom, and, where the meat was too thick, slashed it with their knives so that the juice would come out. After that, the women helped to pound the carcass with stones, and at last the men trampled it underfoot to squeeze out the last of the juice. By then, the others were up. She saw Iwanchou standing nearby, pretending to watch the work. She did not look at him.

When they had finished trampling the carcass underfoot, the men took the sides of moose and stretched them on poles over the fires. The smoking began. Neehatin came out, eating scraps from last night's feast and calling the orders. The sleds were to be loaded and the children and women must start back across this island to the place where the canoes were beached. So we are going on, she thought. She looked for the Blackrobe and saw him sitting on a bundle of his belongings, peering, as he often did, at a small charm which he carried with him. It was covered in a black skin and was made of white strips of bark sewn together. On the white bark were signs painted with a black stick. Were they ornaments? She had asked Iwanchou, but he made some stupid joke. He said the Blackrobe heard men speak when he looked at the black signs on the bark. Now, as she watched the Blackrobe, she saw he had the shaking sickness. If the Blackrobe died, what would Iwanchou do? Where would he go? She felt afraid. Hurriedly she loaded her bark sled and then helped load the sled of her little brother. She went off with the first group, the younger women and children. The men were still smoking the moose. Later, they would fold it and bind it in packages and haul it to the canoes. As she left, she heard her father, Chomina, call out that he would form a party of hunters. There might be porcupine or beaver, he said. She heard Neehatin joke that her father pretended to hunt so that he would not have to carry his share of burdens. Her father did not like such jokes.

As she went along the edge of the trees, she heard the forest speak. She listened but did not catch it. She asked her little brother, Outiji, "Did you hear what it said?"

"It said there is a storm," her little brother told her.

She did not know if she believed him. He was at an age when he wanted to be a man and always had an answer.

When they reached the canoes, the sun was still high. It was a cold winter sun, which did not melt the snow. Her mother told her to help reload the canoes. "But we are not paddling now, are we?" she said. "It's late."

"The bentback has told Neehatin we must go at once," her mother said.

The men, including the hunters, came into camp as the women began loading. They brought extra bundles and also the dried moose. When the canoes were loaded, Neehatin told them to put them in the water.

"Oh, shit," her cousin said. "That means we'll be building the habitation after the sun dies. What the fuck is going on?"

"Shut up," her aunt said. "Get in the canoe."

On the river, they began to sing; it passed the time. But Neehatin stood and called that they be silent. She looked back at the canoe where Iwanchou was the rear paddler. Did he know what that meant? Would anyone tell him? She saw the Blackrobe paddling in his awkward way. The bentback sorcerer sat facing him. Again, she felt afraid. A wind rushed up the river. It cried like a dying woman.

"I told you," her little brother said. "Here comes the storm."

▼

It snowed. Not as it had snowed the days before, but a blinding wall of white driven by great northern winds, so that the air about them howled and swirled and the canoes stalled in the water like paper boats. They were forced to land. They landed on a thickly wooded river-bank, where the trees came down to the water's edge. They dragged the canoes through thick snow in which they sank up to their thighs before donning snowshoes. The storm lashed the trees, causing them to make a sound like cannon. The dogs, howling in discomfort, scampered up the snowbank and hid in the forest. But there was no real shelter, not even in the great vaults of birch and spruce. The Algonkin, with the weary tenacity of felons performing a penitential task, dragged out their birch-bark roofing, hacked at branches and in a make-shift yet deliberate way cleared a shallow space in the snow. Then, huddling in a human wall, they built a fire amid the swirling drifts. The poles were thrown up in a loose circle, and the birch bark was assembled and tied down to form a makeshift roof. By the time darkness came, all huddled around the fire in the insufficient habi-tation. Outside, the winter howled and the trees, groan-ing under the weight of snow, shook and swayed until heavy branches crashed into the white silence of the ground below. Toward dawn the storm died. At dawn a woman gave birth to a baby four months before its time. In the huddled confines of the habitation, the infant was brought forth amid the groans of wakened sleepers, its bloodied body, severed from the afterbirth, held up over the dying fire as its mother perfunctorily slapped it to see if it lived. It did not. She crawled to the entrance and went toward the forest where, high in a tree, away from the dogs, she laid the small slime-covered corpse in a crook between the branches. As she went back to the habitation, the Blackrobe passed her. She thought he had come out to piss, but, as she watched, he went to the place where she had left the baby. He took down the corpse, put a handful of snow in his own mouth, then spit the snow water into his palm and trickled it over the tiny face. She heard him say something in the Norman tongue.

She watched the baby. It was dead. He took the corpse and put it back where she had laid it, high in the tree. He touched his hand to his brow, then in turn to each shoulder. He looked sick, as though he would fall down. She turned and went back into the habitation. When she crawled close to her husband, she told him what she had seen. Together they watched the Blackrobe crawl in again and lie down beside the sorcerer. Had the Blackrobe put a spell on her so that the child came before its time? She asked this of her husband, but he did not answer. She felt empty and weary and afraid. Her husband held her in his arms. Within a short time they heard the call to rise and go on.

▼

Outside the habitation, Chomina passed a small piece of smoked meat to each man, woman and child. The habitation was disassembled and the canoes were dragged down to the river. As Laforgue helped, pulling a canoe, Daniel came up and took him aside.

"Are you ill, Father Paul?"

"I had a fever," Laforgue said. "But last night it broke. I am better now."

"It will be hard paddling," Daniel said. "I heard Ougebemat say that for four days they will be in an area of great danger. That means hostile Savages. They want to get through as quickly as they can."

"What people live in this part of the river?"

"I don't know. Father, I am sorry about what I said to you. If we are going into danger, we must not be enemies."

"We are not enemies," Laforgue said. "But we must talk about these things. Nothing is more important than that."

"We cannot talk now. Besides, I don't know what to say." Suddenly the boy stared at Laforgue. "Father, what's the matter?"

"My ear," Laforgue said. He put his hand over his right ear, bent forward, then collapsed in the snow. Rolling over, he looked up at the boy. The boy's lips were moving. Oh, my God, Laforgue said to himself. Have I gone completely deaf? The ringing sound shut out all others as the boy helped him to his feet.

Then, as suddenly as it had started, the ringing ceased. Laforgue heard the boy ask, "Father Paul? Father Paul?"

"It's all right," Laforgue said. "I have these spells. They pass."

"You are ill. You are not fit to travel."

"I am stronger than you think," Laforgue said.

He heard the Savages calling his name. "Nicanis? Nicanis?"

"Don't try to paddle," the boy said. "It is too much for you. I will tell Neehatin that you are sick."

"No, you won't. I will paddle. Don't tell him." La-

forgue turned and ran down to the waiting canoe, lifting
his cassock as he waded into the icy water. When the
canoe moved out, forming part of a snake which glided
along the river, again he heard the telltale ringing. He
looked at the sorcerer, who sat with the children on the
bundles stacked in the middle of the canoe. The sorcerer
was talking to the children, but Laforgue could not hear
him. The ringing stopped. He heard voices, clearly, and
the slap of his paddle in the water. It was as though some
abscess in his ear had burst. He heard as he had not
heard in weeks. And in that moment of deliverance, he
saw Neehatin half rise in the canoe ahead and make a
gesture with his hand. The Savages fell silent. The
stroke increased to a pace which made Laforgue break
into a sweat. But the sweat was the sweat of toil, not
fever. His fever had broken. His hearing seemed restored. *O Lord,* he prayed, *Thou hast given me back my
ears and my strength. Thou hast shown me that through
Thy hand, I am capable of feats I had not believed to be
in this body of mine. If it be Thy wish that I suffer
greater privations in the days ahead, I welcome it. Thou
hast given me this cross for Thy honor and for the salvation of these poor barbarians. I thank Thee.*

And there, among the faint sounds of the river, the
slap of paddles, the canoes gliding through the chill
morning mists, he was filled with a strange exaltation. In
France, in the cloister, after a long and painful night's
vigil of prayer, or at humble or disgusting tasks in the
kitchens and sickrooms of the Order, he had, on rare occasions, known this feeling. It was as though Paul Laforgue no longer existed on this earth but, instead, a
body and mind made for Jesus did Jesus' will. And this

morning that calm he had known in former days seemed as nothing compared with the exaltation he now felt in this wilderness, surrounded by Savages who drove on as though possessed. Everything that he did, everything that he suffered, he did and suffered as a Jesuit, for the greater glory of God. God had tested him and would test him further. God had restored his hearing to remind him he was not alone.

God is with me. God honors me with this task.

6

On the third day of their race through the place of darkness, Neehatin saw the White Face Mountain. He had driven his people hard. That night, he asked men as well as women to help assemble the habitation. All moved like old ones, they were so weary from the paddling. But the habitation was well built. When the last of the smoked moose meat had served as the evening meal, all were drowsy before the fires. They would soon sleep. Neehatin beckoned to the senior men to lie close to him and brought out tobacco.

"Shit," said Amantacha. "Where did you find this?"

All were smiling. Tobacco was loved as much as food.

"I forgot it," Neehatin lied. "I put it among the beaver skins, and then I forgot it." He filled their pipes, then passed back the rest of the tobacco to the older women and the young men. He offered a pipeful to the young Norman, who refused, as did the Blackrobe. The sorcerer, smoking from a curved pipe of his own making, curled up like a child at Neehatin's feet as Neehatin peered across the smoking fires to make sure the Norman boy was not in hearing. Then he asked the sorcerer, "Do you tell me new things about my dream?"

"It has not yet been told to me," the sorcerer said.

"Then you do not yet know who is the fish?"

He wanted to press this little shit for an answer. For he knew the bentback. He would wait until Neehatin had spoken, then claim his wisdom for himself.

"No," said the sorcerer. "It has not yet been told to me who is the fish."

"When will you know?" Neehatin said. He wanted to be sure that all heard, including Chomina.

"It will come," said the sorcerer.

"Shit," said Ougebemat. He was happy. "This tobacco is good stuff."

"I am smoking," said old Awandouie. It was his way of saying thanks. The others said the "Ho, ho" of approval. Neehatin smiled. He was glad he had held this tobacco in reserve. They were grateful. They would heed his counsel.

"In the dream," Neehatin said, "the fish swam up to me and led me to the farther shore. Tomorrow night we will reach that shore."

"But who is the fish?" asked the bentback. "That is the question."

"You are the fish," Neehatin said. "That is why you did not know the answer."

"What are you talking about?" Chomina said. He lay on his back with his knees drawn up, sucking on his pipe with long grateful puffs.

"Mestigoit is the fish we have taken with us through the dark place. He has driven the demon out of the Blackrobe. The Blackrobe has lost his power. He cannot cast a spell on us any more."

"But how do you know?" Chomina said. He turned and looked at Neehatin as he said it.

"Today, as I paddled my canoe," Neehatin said, "the forest spoke. It said, *Mestigoit is the fish who helps us. He has saved us from danger*, it said." Neehatin looked down at the bentback curled up at his feet. "We must give you a good present, you little asshole," he said, and laughed.

"But we are still in the danger," Chomina warned.

"Not for long. Tomorrow night we reach the Great Rapids."

"The rapids are more than a night's paddling."

"Not so," Neehatin said. "We have passed the White Face Mountain. We are still in danger, but at the rapids we will leave the boy and the Blackrobe and send them on alone. We ourselves will cross the river to the other shore and go to the winter hunting place. We will be safe."

"Alone?" said old Awandouie. "The Normans will die. They will never manage the portage up the rapids."

"The Blackrobe is stronger than he looks," Neehatin said. "Last night in my dream he walked alone into a village in the Huron country."

"Some fucking dream," said Chomina, and the others laughed.

"I dreamed it," Neehatin said. He did not smile. In the smoky habitation a dog barked, a child cried. The senior men said nothing.

"He walked into a village," Neehatin said. "The village was empty. No people. No people at all."

Again, a dog barked.

"If you dreamed it, it will come to pass," said Ougebemat. "But will the Norman chief absolve us from our promise because you tell him you had a dream?"

"They gave us six fucking muskets and a little powder," Neehatin said. "And four axes and some awls. And beads and other shit."

"And two iron kettles," said Chomina.

"All right, two fucking kettles. Presents, good presents. All right. But, for that, in the last four days we came into the danger. We are still in it. Everyone here could die. Fuck the Normans. We will take them to the rapids. What more do they want?"

"We gave our word that day in the stone habitation of Agnonha," Chomina said. "You and I, both. We said we would take them to the rapids, then send two men up the rapids with them and on to the place where they meet the Allumette. You know what that fucker Agnonha is like. He won't forget it if you try to screw him."

"Sometimes," Neehatin said, "I wonder if you think with your head or your ass. You tell me that if we leave them at the foot of the rapids, they are dead men. Now you tell me we should be afraid that these dead men will report back to Québec."

"That's right," Ougebemat said. "We will say we

sent two men up with them. Who's to know the differ-ence? Agnonha doesn't keep count of every fucking Al-gonkin. How could he?"

"And even if the Blackrobe survives to reach the Huron land," Amantacha said, "it will be another winter before he can send back any word to Québec."

"So we are agreed, then?" Neehatin asked. "We have risked enough for their fucking presents. We leave them at the rapids."

The others nodded. But not Chomina. "Shit," Chomina said. "I am not afraid of any Norman chief. You all know that. But the musket which Agnonha gave to me, I will give it to one of the young men if he will go up the rapids with the Blackrobe. It will only be a journey of—what—three nights? Then he can come down again, take a canoe and rejoin us in the winter hunting place."

"Easy. Nothing to it," Neehatin said, and laughed. "But I notice you don't want to go yourself."

"Asshole. I have a family," Chomina said. "I would have to take them with me up the rapids. That's why I don't want to go. But we gave a promise. We told Ag-nonha we would take Nicanis to the head of the rapids."

"Fuck the promise," Neehatin said. He looked around and saw uncertainty in some eyes. He looked at the sorcerer. The bentback hated Normans. "What do you say, Mestigoit?" he asked.

"I say we should follow the dream. The dream is stronger than any promise. You have dreamed that the Blackrobe walks alone in a Huron village. So he will walk there. Obey the dream."

The others gave the guttural of assent. Neehatin looked at the bentback and, for once, was glad he had brought him along. But Chomina took his pipe from his mouth and spat in the fire. "Now it is the rest of you who are thinking with your assholes," Chomina said. "The Blackrobe can only walk into that village with our help. Can you see that boy and the Blackrobe reaching the high place alone? Of course not. We must go with them. That is what the dream says. Don't you see?"

"I see that you are afraid of these wooden islanders," Neehatin said, smiling to negate the insult.

"I am not afraid," Chomina said. "But we have begun to need their trade. That is our undoing, and it will be our ending."

"We are not talking of that," Neehatin said. "I am saying that unless we dump the Blackrobe tomorrow night, every man, woman and child among us could die."

"I am not talking about risking all our lives," Chomina said. "I am talking about sending a young warrior who wants to earn a musket. That's what *I* am talking about."

"All right, I ask the council." Neehatin rolled over on his back and stared at the other faces. "Do we put this to the young men or not?"

"I say no. I say fuck the Normans," Ougebemat said. "What does Awandouie say?"

All looked now to the oldest man in council. He had lived sixty winters, maybe more. His was the memory of former dangers. "If Neehatin's dream sees the Blackrobe in a Huron village, then the Blackrobe will reach that village. In Neehatin's dream the village is empty. The Blackrobe walks alone. Not with Chomina, not with any of our men. Obey the dream."

Neehatin watched Chomina, then said, "Do all agree?"

"Just remember," Chomina said. "Agnonha will cut

our balls off when he finds out about this." He laughed
to show that he was joking. The other men laughed too
but looked to Neehatin.

"Then we ditch the hairy ones tomorrow night,"
Neehatin said. "Are we agreed?"

"The council is agreed," said Awandouie.

▼

It had ceased to snow. The freezing cold which had
numbed Laforgue's feet these past two days was replaced by a mild breeze. The sun shone as though in this
capricious wilderness the summer of flies and heat might
again return to vanquish the approaching winter. Birds
sang as the snake of canoes set off at its usual fast, gliding
pace. Laforgue, paddling with an ease he would not have
believed possible two weeks ago, felt a new vigor in his
shoulders and arms. This morning, as the canoes were
being loaded, Neehatin had said, "We will travel far
today, Nicanis. But soon we will rest."

"How many days are we from the rapids?"

Neehatin thought for a moment. "Two nights,
maybe less. We have made good time."

Shortly after noon, the silence of the paddlers was
broken by a murmur of whispered excitement as the
Savages looked down and saw ripples in the water. The
hunchback, who, as usual, sat cross-legged on a heap of
bundles facing Laforgue, bent to whisper in the priest's
ear. "White water," the hunchback said. "We have traveled as fast as wet shit through a bumhole." He grinned
in glee.

"What do you mean?"

"Shh," the hunchback said and looked with glittering eyes at the shore. "White water. Two hours. The rapids."

"But Neehatin said two nights."

"Shh." Again the hunchback peered at the shore as though afraid of being overheard. "Soon. Two hours. You'll see."

The canoes moved on. As was their custom the Savages did not stop to rest, and in early afternoon, as the sun began to dip in the sky, Laforgue saw myriad currents as they glided over stony shallows. Suddenly, Neehatin's canoe veered away. The other canoes balanced on the shallow rippling tide of river as Neehatin's craft went in to shore and the leader leaped out. He held a hatchet in one hand. Donning his snowshoes, he hurried across a thick carpet of snow, into a clearing. It was then that Laforgue saw signs of foot tracks and, in a circular place, cleared of snow, the remains of a fire. Neehatin went quickly to this dead fire, knelt, picked up charred embers, sniffed them, then looked about. In the other canoes, men, women and children, silent, stared at the shore as though they had seen something dread. Their leader, turning, ran back to the river and boarded his canoe, which at once swung out from shore. The other canoes, as though impatient to depart, circled in behind it. Swiftly, Neehatin's canoe forged again into its lead position. The paddlers bent to their task. The canoes fled on.

Laforgue, paddling, said a prayer. Was that fire a sign of the hostile Savages Daniel had spoken of two days back? The waters around them grew more turbulent. After less than an hour, Laforgue saw ahead, majestic in their white confusion, the Great Rapids of which Father Bourque had spoken. Here they would leave this band of Savages and, with two paddlers, portage to a higher point in the falls and continue their journey with two canoes. He looked over at Daniel's canoe. The boy, paddling at the prow, was staring about him, as though, like the Savages, he knew he ventured into a dangerous place. The canoes, stalled by the rapids, made slow progress until, at a widening of the river, Neehatin gave the signal to land.

All canoes were pulled up on the riverbank, but as soon as the Savages landed Laforgue noticed that they did not go about their usual tasks. Instead, mothers curbed their children, warning them to be quiet, and for once the unruly children seemed willing to obey. The dogs ran about sniffing, urinating on tree trunks, but when one of them attacked another and began to bark, one of the Savages at once felled it with a blow from his club. Laforgue saw Neehatin point to five of the hunters, who at once took up bows, arrows and hatchets and set off cautiously into the surrounding woods. Then the Algonkian leader went to the women and children. He spoke to them in low tones. At once, about half the women set about cutting pine branches for a habitation. The others did not assist. Laforgue saw Daniel, standing alone, staring at this scene. He went to the boy.

"What's happening? Do you know?"

"They are afraid," the boy said. "Something is worrying them. They will not talk to me. What are they doing down there at the canoes?"

"Those are our canoes," Laforgue said.

Among the beached canoes, three of the older

women were moving bundles from one craft to another. "Those are our goods," Laforgue said.

Hurrying, he and Daniel went down to the canoes.

"What are you doing?" Daniel asked a woman.

"These are your things," the woman said. "We don't want to mix our shit with yours." She laughed, and the women with her laughed also.

"Come on," Daniel said, smiling at her. "Tell me what you're really doing."

"Ask Neehatin," the woman said.

Laforgue turned away. "Let's go. I will speak to Neehatin."

But as they went back up the riverbank they saw the Savages watching the forest. Through the trees, running lightly, came the five hunters whom Neehatin had dispatched. One of them held a large bird which he had killed with an arrow. He pulled the arrow clear as he handed the bird to Neehatin. The women who had cut branches for the habitation abruptly ceased their work. No one spoke. Ougebemat raised his hatchet and made a circular movement. Immediately, all the Algonkian men, women and children ran back to their boats, leaving Neehatin alone in the clearing with Daniel and Laforgue.

"What is happening?" Laforgue said to the Algonkian leader.

Neehatin smiled. He held out the freshly killed bird. "Here," he said. "This is for you. Tonight, you will eat. You will truly eat."

Laforgue did not take the bird. "You have not answered me," he said.

Neehatin threw the bird on the snow. "So you refuse my gift?" He no longer smiled.

"We do not refuse it," Daniel said and at once picked it up. "We thank you, Neehatin."

Laforgue turned and looked back at the canoes. The Savages were pushing them over the snow, going back down to the river. All but two canoes, those in which the Jesuit supplies were loaded.

"So," Laforgue said. "We have reached the rapids. Who are the paddlers who will take us on to the Huron lands?"

"What paddlers?" Neehatin said. "You don't need paddlers. Your sorcery will take you up the portage."

"You made a promise to Agnonha," Laforgue said. "Two men to guide us."

"You're full of shit, Nicanis," Neehatin said and laughed, a wild laugh, which he quickly curbed, looking back at the trees.

"You made a promise," Laforgue said again. "You gave your word."

"The branches are cut for your habitation and the ground is cleared," Neehatin said. "But do not camp here for more than one night. And throw out half of that shit you have in the canoes if you want to reach the upper rapids without going back and forth six or seven journeys." He turned away and walked down to the waiting canoes.

Laforgue watched him go. He remembered his days in the cloister, when he had read with excitement and dread of how Father Brabant had been abandoned at this point by Savages who had accepted presents and promised to accompany him. He felt a strange calm, the calm of knowing the worst.

Suddenly, without a word, Daniel ran down to the

river, wading into the water, going toward Chomina's canoe. Laforgue saw the girl at the rear of the craft and Chomina's wife and little boy sitting in the center. Daniel spoke, not to the girl but to Chomina himself, whereupon Chomina shook his head and waved him off. At that moment, Neehatin reached his canoe, leaping into it like a cat. Chomina at once took up his paddle, and he and his men steered their craft out into the stream, leaving Daniel standing abandoned in the shallows. The canoes circled and turned downriver. Chomina's daughter did not look back. In a moment the canoes had rounded the bend in the river and were gone.

The boy, splashing in the shallows, climbed the riverbank, coming toward Laforgue. I will be gentle with him, Laforgue decided. I will pretend that he did not want to leave me. But, as he watched, the boy ran floundering in the snow toward the two canoes which had been left behind. In frantic, awkward haste he began to remove from one the bundles tied in skins which contained the provisions, mass vestments, books and other necessities for the Huron mission. When these bundles lay on the snow, the boy pushed the light craft down to the river and settled it in the water. He did not look at Laforgue but jumped in the canoe and paddled it out into the stream, circling, following the direction of the Algonkin, a solitary, driven figure, the light, half-empty canoe skimming like a flat stone over the shallow white waters of the rapids. In a moment he had reached the river bend.

Laforgue looked down at the dead bird at his feet, then at the pine branches cut for his night's habitation. He was alone.

It was still two hours to darkness. In the oilskin package which contained his map was a notebook in which Father Gulot and Father Brabant had set down their cautions and advice. Both priests had suffered abandonment and had survived. Laforgue, sitting on one of the bundles left in the snow by Daniel, opened the small book and read, in Father Gulot's neat handwriting, instructions on how to light a fire and protect it. In the same book Father Brabant had drawn a plan showing the construction of a simple shelter, and as Laforgue thumbed through the pages he decided that this would be his first task.

Working with surprising speed, he cleared a small patch of ground and laid down the branches already cut by the Algonkian women. He then erected a triangular covering on which he spread the sheets of birch bark which he found in the rear of the canoe. When he had finished, he lit a small fire and began to pluck the bird's feathers. He filled the kettle with handfuls of snow, planning to boil the bird. He did not think beyond each task but worked as he had seen the Savages work, with single-minded attention. He cleaned the bird, something which the Savages did not do, then put it in the boiling pot. He looked at the night sky, which was cloudy. He could not see a moon.

A light rain began to fall and, remembering that the bundles from the second canoe lay unprotected in the snow, he left his fire and dragged them back into the shelter of the forest. Tomorrow, when he traveled on, he would be unable to carry even a fraction of the contents of their two canoes up the long and arduous portages described by Father Brabant. He must take the minimum and bury or hide the rest until spring, when it could be reclaimed.

It was then, as he dragged the bundles into the forest, that he discovered at the base of a huge tree a space like a cave where the snow had not penetrated. The space was big enough to hold two men. It was dry and clean, covered with pine needles. He crawled into it. It was a cache where he might hide the mass vestments, the missals and the chalice, which he could no longer carry. In the morning he would rearrange all these things. He then realized that, weary as he was, he had no appetite for the bird now in the pot and that if he drew his heavy cloak about him in this sheltered cave he would sleep more snugly than in the rough habitation out there in the snows. Accordingly, he left the bundles by the tree trunk to mark the spot and returned to his fire, removing the kettle and setting it to one side. Then, taking his cloak and piling the other bundles beside the loaded canoe, he reentered the forest, found his cave under the tree trunk, crawled in and lay curled up in his cloak. He thought of Daniel and said a prayer. *O Lord, do not abandon him. Succor him as Thou hast succored me.*

He slept. Outside his tree cave the night rainfall became a downpour, a rain which melted the snows, revealing again the earth's autumnal covering of leaves and moss. The noise of the rain did not rouse him, but sometime in the darkness of the hour before dawn, he was jerked into wakefulness by another sound. Voices.

Savages: close, very close. They have come back. If they have come back, then Daniel is with them.

Relief flooded him, making him feel almost faint. What were they saying? He crawled to the mouth of his cave, slipping off his cloak.

The voices spoke a strange dialect, kin to the Huron tongue.

"No, shit no. They wouldn't leave their peltries, would they?"

A second voice said, "Why would they build this shelter that wouldn't cover a dead hare?"

Cautiously he put his head out. The small guttering fire he had built had been replaced by a larger one. Around it, eating from his kettle, sat five or six Savages, all males. On their knees or at their feet were clubs, hatchets and bows. In the firelight their faces gleamed with paint, colored red, yellow and blue. Their hair was cut and braided in strange patterns; they wore ornaments of teeth and shells.

"They are sorcerers," said a voice from outside the firelight, and at that moment two other Savages came up from the river. Behind their astonishing facial masks, their mouths were wide in laughter. One of them, the taller, was wearing, backward, the white mass vestments of silk and cloth of gold Laforgue was taking to the Huron mission. The sight of this Savage, his skull shaved, clothed in the blessed garments sewn for the mission by the nuns of the Abbaye aux Dames at Caen, seemed like a scene from some ugly dream. The other Savage who came up from the boats held out the precious flagon of sacramental wine.

"Norman drink," shouted one of those sitting at the fire. All rose, laughing, as the flagon was passed around. Although it was a two-gallon flagon, the Savages disposed of it in one round of swilling gulps.

"Norman sorcerers," said one of the strangers. "No Algonkin would carry this drink for days without sucking it down. They are Normans, these pricks."

"That's why they don't build a proper habitation," another said. "Blackrobes, I bet."

"Yes, Blackrobes."

"Then where are they? Did they have two canoes and take one of them? Or did they run off in the woods when they saw us coming?"

"Agariata, you are full of shit. How could they hear us or see us when we came up like shadows?"

"Then why did they leave their food and canoe?"

"Algonkin brought them here. That's what I think."

"Then where are those pricks of Algonkin?"

"Across the river, no?"

"Is there more of that fucking drink? I want more."

"Look in the canoe."

He heard them whooping, as they ran down to the riverbank, heard them talking down there, but not what they said. There was no more wine, he knew, and soon they came back. One of them was now wearing his spare cassock as a cloak. As they came back to the fire, the hideously painted Savage faces were solemn as icons. They spoke in low voices.

". . . and wrong, fucking wrong."

"Algonkin . . ."

"No, wait. Those pricks did not bury this stuff. Therefore they have carried other stuff up to the first portage stop. Tomorrow they will come down again and pick up this lot."

"We'll wait. . . ."

"Fucking right. At the fork we can see both the river and the trail."

He heard them approach. He ducked his head back down into his hiding place, heard their soft shoes on the rain-sodden leaves outside. The footsteps passed. All was silent. He lay, listening, but heard nothing. Two hours later, a cold sun rose over the river. Birds sang. Melting snow dripped from the branches overhead. Laforgue crept to the opening of his tree-trunk cave and peered out. There was no sign of the strange Savages, but he knew that they were out there, waiting. He was trapped.

7

Neehatin looked back and saw the Norman boy, Iwanchou, in an empty canoe, gaining. Shit! He looked at his wife. She met his eye. She was the one who had said Annuka, Chomina's daughter, was fucking with this boy. And it was true. That is why he ran to Chomina's canoe. What will I do? If I let him come with us to the winter hunting place, we will have a witness who can tell Agnonha what we have done today. But if I put a hatchet in his head and someone betrays me, Agnonha will train his arquebuses on all the Algonkin until I come forward to confess. Then he will kill me. Shit! It's Chomina's fault. He made a friend of that boy. Now we must pay for that stupidity.

Iwanchou's canoe joined the snake. Neehatin turned and waved to the boy. He needed time. He looked at the forest but the forest was silent. He signaled to his wife to come to the rear of the canoe, and, as though she had been expecting this, she at once put up her paddle and crawled close. He bent to whisper. No one must know that he sought counsel from his woman.

"What do you see?"

She closed her eyes and rocked to and fro. "I don't see."

"Try. We are in shit."

"I know, I know."

She stopped rocking. She opened her eyes and looked at him. "Send the boy back.'

"How can I? Even if I lift a hatchet to put in his skull, he will not go back now. He has left the Blackrobe. There is no going back."

"He will go back."

"Fuck off," Neehatin said, and laughed. He did not understand her, he never understood her, but he believed her. He had always been right to believe her.

She smiled. She crawled back down the canoe and, taking up her paddle, fell in with the others as they stroked. Neehatin rose and gave the signal for the fastest pace. He had just seen the beaver rock on the far shore. Soon they would leave the canoes and go inland. It was usually permitted to go through that place to reach the winter hunting. The enemy often allowed it. But not always.

When he came to the place of landing, he set his canoe in and passed out word that no one was to talk. The Norman boy disembarked with the others. Neehatin did not speak to him but did not stop him from helping as the people prepared sleds and loaded all their belongings. The canoes were carried on shore and placed in the higher forks of trees, then covered with cut branches. Chomina came up.

"What about this Iwanchou?" Chomina asked.

"What about him? You tell me. Your daughter is a bitch in heat, and he runs after her."

Chomina laughed as though this were a joke. "Shit," he said. "He came after us because he doesn't want to die. Who can blame him?"

"Let's go," Neehatin said. "We can talk when we're out of the corridor."

Amantacha came up and nodded to show his group was ready. "If we see beaver or porcupine?" he whispered.

"Kill," Neehatin told him. "But don't delay and don't go out of the corridor."

Ougebemat came up. "Ready," he said.

The Norman boy now approached. Neehatin knew he waited his chance to speak. He pointed to the boy. "Go with Chomina. We will talk later."

"Neehatin?" the boy began.

"Quiet," Neehatin said. He turned away.

The people had made long sleds of bark, cut narrow because they must be dragged between the trees. Although the snow had half melted in this place, snowshoes were worn. To remain in the corridor, they must stay in the woods, bending down to pass under half fallen trees, stepping over large branches which had fallen on the ground. Even the children were burdened, but on this journey the men, not the women and children, went ahead. All were silent. Even the dogs seemed aware of the danger.

After the first hour, the party came into drifts of snow in which, despite snowshoes, they sank up to their knees. Neehatin gave the order that they rest. After some minutes they again set out. They saw no game, but when they were almost at the end of the corridor and coming toward the safe place, Amantacha's son found and killed a porcupine while Ougebemat, coming on a small river, found a beaver dam and killed eight before the beavers swam into a hiding place from which they could not be extricated. Neehatin reflected that there would be meat to supplement the sagamité tonight. Does that mean our fortunes have improved since we dumped the Blackrobe? Or is this a false moment of peace?

He looked up and saw, above the trees, the side of a small mountain. It meant that they had less than an hour to go. He signaled to Ougebemat and the others; then, whispering to Chomina to take the lead, he fell back, waiting until the women and children caught up. As he watched the women approach through the trees, he saw his wife among them. She dragged a sled long as two men, the halter around her forehead straining as though it would break. Neehatin came up to her and, dragging his own sled, pulled a cord around hers to help her with her heavy burden.

"What do you see?" he asked in a low voice.

She shut her eyes and did not answer.

"Say it," he whispered. "Even if it's bad."

"Send Iwanchou back."

"Why?"

"I see him with blood on his face. Send him back."

"Blood?" His whisper seemed to echo in the surrounding forest. "Could it be blood caused by my hatchet?"

She shook her head. She trudged on beside him, silent, her breathing hoarse as a dog's as she dragged her sled through the snows. At last she looked up and saw the clear place beyond the trees, the end of the corridor, the place where they would be free to rest. She looked at her husband. "Now," she said. "Do it now. Send him back."

When they reached the safe place, the Algonkin threw down their burdens and, laughing, making their usual jokes, ran about in the snow, hopping like seabirds in their large round snowshoes. If the hunting was good in this place, they would not have to move for several days. In the next two months in the winter hunting place they could travel without fear of enemies. But there were some who did not take part in the general merriment. Chomina stood with his wife, watching the Norman boy as the boy spoke earnestly with Annuka, their daughter. Neehatin watched Chomina watch the boy.

"We will begin the habitation," Amantacha said.

"No," Neehatin said. "Call the senior men. We must talk."

"What is he saying to her?" Chomina asked his wife.

"He has put a spell on her," Chomina's wife said. "She wants us to take him as one of our family."

"It's not a spell, it's his prick," Chomina said, and laughed, although he was far from laughter.

The sorcerer came up to him. "Neehatin wants a council."

As the rest of the party went about the tasks for making camp, Neehatin led the senior men to a quiet spot. "The subject is the Norman," he told them.

"I have been thinking about that," Ougebemat said.

"I too," said Awandouie. "When the winter is over, Iwanchou will find his own people. He will say what we have done today. And we will be fucked. We will have Agnonha to deal with."

"Exactly," Neehatin said. "So what is your advice?"

"Send him back to the Blackrobe," said Amantacha.

"How can we do that? What if he does not go? What if he goes back down the great river and reaches Québec? As long as he is alive, he is a danger to us."

"Neehatin is right," said Ougebemat. "Let's put a hatchet in his head. Now."

"Whose hatchet?" Neehatin said.

"Yours. You are our leader."

"Mine? Fuck you. The man who puts a hatchet in Iwanchou's head is the man Agnonha will hunt down."

"Agnonha will never know," Amantacha said. "We are all friends here."

"Even so, Neehatin is right," old Awandouie cautioned. "Five winters from now, if some woman or child among us speaks with a loose tongue and tells what happened here, Neehatin is a dead man."

"Shit," said Ougebemat. "That's right."

"It's your fault," Neehatin said to Chomina. "That daughter of yours is why that young prick followed us."

"I see," Chomina said. "It is my fault that I have a daughter. But is it my fault that you broke our promise to Agnonha? If we had kept our word and sent two men up the rapids with the Blackrobe, we would be happy to-night."

"Would we? With two of our men up there on the portage? Two who might never come back?"

"We gave our word," Chomina said. "If we weren't going to keep our word, we shouldn't have taken Agnonha's presents. We have become as bad as the Normans themselves. All we think of is things. We have become greedy and stupid like the hairy ones."

"Yes, that is true," said Awandouie. "Perhaps that is how the Normans will destroy us. Not in war, but by a spell that makes us like them."

"That is shit," Neehatin said, and laughed to show he was not angry. "Look, you assholes, let's not have any bad words now. We have reached the hunting place. We are safe. We have meat to eat tonight. I'm going to send that boy back to Nicanis. I'll tell him that unless he leaves tomorrow, he'll get a present from me: a hatchet in his skull."

"But if he refuses to go," Amantacha said, "you're back in the shit. We've just said it's too risky to kill him."

"Wait," Chomina said. "I can solve this riddle."

Neehatin felt a twinge of alarm. Was this an attempt to take over his role as leader?

"I will go back with him," Chomina said.

"You're crazy," Ougebemat said. "That boy doesn't want to go back any more than you do."

"He wants to be part of my family," Chomina said. "I will go with my family, and he will follow us. We will find the Blackrobe and take them both to the top of the rapids, as promised. Annuka and my wife will help with the portages. When we reach the top of the rapids, I will have kept my promise to Agnonha. What the boy and the Blackrobe do after that is none of our business."

"But, fuck it," Ougebemat said. "You are one of us. Why should we let you risk your family for some fucking Normans?"

"Because I made a stupid promise through my own greed," Chomina said. "And now I am stupid enough to keep that promise. Let's get the kettles on. I am hungry. And after tomorrow, I see a few hungry days for me and mine."

"Well, Neehatin," old Awandouie asked. "What do you say to this?"

"I say Chomina has saved our fucking necks," Neehatin said, laughing. He embraced Chomina. As he hugged Chomina he thought of his wife's advice. We are doing what she said we must do. We are sending the boy back. She has the gift of seeing, all right. But who would have thought it would come out like this?

"Then are all agreed that Chomina make this journey?" Awandouie asked. "Those who do not agree, speak now."

No one spoke.

▼

She watched Iwanchou as he worked with the other men, clearing ground for the habitation, using his snowshoe as a shovel, piling the cleared snow into a wall, as he had been taught by her people. As she watched him, she worked with the women on the edge of the clearing, cutting boughs and trimming them. He had not spoken to her since that moment when, heartsick, she paddled away, leaving him behind with the Blackrobe. Even then she had known that it was not finished between them.

Minutes later, when, paddling an empty canoe, he came into sight behind them, her mother asked, "Did you tell him to come?"

"No."

"You are sure?"

"Of course I am sure."

"Then don't speak to him when we land. If you do, we will be blamed."

So she had kept away, although it was as cruel as beating a child. If she did not go to him, he would not come to her. That was a promise between them, made long ago. But now, as the group of senior men came back from their meeting, she saw her father leave the others and go up to Iwanchou. Despite herself she stopped cutting branches and stood, trying to hear what was said. But they were too far away. She remembered what her father had said earlier, when Iwanchou had tried to board their canoe. "Go away. Go back to your own people." And Iwanchou had said, "You are my people now." It was then that he had looked at her. And it was then that she knew she could not give him up.

She set to work again, tying up a bundle of branches, then dragging it across the clearing. As she did this she was able to come closer to her father and Iwanchou. Iwanchou was smiling. Why? Surely the council had not agreed to let him stay? Even though she knew this could not be, her hopes rose, making her almost dizzy. He had a musket, which was something few men possessed. He could kill with it as none of them had yet learned to do. With his musket he would be a hunter whom all admired. He could be her husband.

But it was not until darkness, the habitation built

and the kettles on the fires, that she learned the truth. They were going back. She, her father, her mother, her little brother, Outiji, and Iwanchou would go to the head of the rapids. There, her father said, they would leave Iwanchou and the Blackrobe and return to rejoin the people.

"But what if he follows us back down again? What if he will not stay with the Blackrobe?"

Her father laughed. "You'd like that, wouldn't you?" he said. "You put a spell on him, didn't you, Annuka?"

She said nothing.

"I promised Agnonha to take them to the head of the rapids," her father said. "What Iwanchou does after that is his business."

"But you like him?" she asked. "You said you liked him."

"What's the matter with you? You are beautiful. All the young men want to fuck with you. You can have anyone as a husband."

"The young men do not have muskets," she said.

Her father laughed. "You are full of shit, my girl," he said. "You think I am stupid, don't you? Maybe I am. I have been saying that you put a spell on him. It's the other way around. He has put a spell on you. What do you care about muskets?"

"A man with a musket is a good hunter, a good husband."

"Let us settle one point now," her father said. "He will *not* be your husband. Now, let's go eat. We will leave at first light tomorrow."

"May I speak to him?"

Her father laughed and, coming to her, embraced

her. "Yes, you may speak to him," he said. "But listen to me. There are other men. Good men. Our men."

"It is you who is full of shit," she said and laughed to show him she was not angry.

"Go on, then," he said, smiling at her.

And so, with her father's permission, at last she could go up to Iwanchou, who sat near the kettles, not eating, but watching, waiting for her to come. As she went in his direction, he rose and left the light of the fires. In the darkness, outside the circle of feasting, she found him and kissed him. "Iwanchou," she said. "Iwanchou." For although she found it strange to say anyone's name like this, it was the Norman custom. He liked to hear her say his name.

"Annuka," he said, kissing her. "You've heard the news?"

"Yes."

"It is as if all my wishes are granted," he said. "If we can take Nicanis up the rapids, then, I think, he can go on alone."

"But you are going with him?"

He shook his head. "I spoke with your father," he said. "He told me that when he has taken us up the rapids, his promise to Agnonha is fulfilled. What I do after that is my affair, he said." He took her in his arms. "So everything is well," he said. "Come. Let's go in the woods for a while."

"No. The kettles are on. We must eat before all the meat is gone."

"I am hungry for you, not for food."

She laughed and pulled free of him. "Later," she said. "I want meat now. We will eat only sagamité in the days ahead."

8

$\mathbf{A}$ lynx, moving as though
at any moment the earth would shift beneath its paws,
came with infinite caution into the clearing where last
night's fire had been guttered by morning showers. Laforgue, who had waited since dawn, wondering if he
dare venture outside his place of concealment, watched
the lynx, his surrogate, as it moved closer to the empty
kettle, its delicate nostrils leading it to the smell of food.
Suddenly, the animal lifted its head, looking around as
though it had heard something and was prepared to bolt.
For a long moment it stood statue-still, then turned its
head so that Laforgue could see its eyes, eyes which did
not see him. Uneasy, as though threatened, the lynx

crouched down, then cautiously began to make its way back in the direction from which it had come. As it did, Laforgue heard a noise like a sigh. The lynx stopped, transfixed, head thrown up. Vibrating like a harp string was a slender arrow embedded in its neck. At once, Laforgue ducked his head down into his hiding place. His ears, which a few days ago had been dulled by infection, now seemed to him like the ears of a Savage in their ability to detect the merest sound. When, again, he risked a look outside, a Savage, one of the strange painted faces of last night, bent over the lynx, removing the arrow. A second Savage crept from the trees and attached thongs to the dead animal's front paws. The first Savage lifted the animal up, placing it on the back of the one who had tied its paws. Both Savages moved away, going up the riverbank to the spot where the rapids, in a rush of white water, became unnavigable. Within seconds they were gone.

They are here and they are waiting. How long will they watch this place? How long before they decide to move on? They have killed a lynx and will want to eat it. For that, they must light a fire. If they light a fire, they will be sure to light it in some place where it cannot be seen. Where? They are waiting in a place where the trail from that first portage passes close by. They can also see the river. What will I do? What can I do?

The hours passed slowly. He watched the sun, fitfully present among high rolling clouds. He watched the river. For a time, he prayed. For a time he lay, staring at the little silver crucifix on the bead rosary his mother had given him on the day of his ordination as a priest. He thought of that day in the church of Saint Ouen, the solemn High Mass, the unseen choir singing the Kyrie high in the vaulted roof, his parents kneeling on prie-dieux just in front of the communion rail, their faces a mirror of their joy. How long ago that seemed, how odd, as though he had read of it in some book, or dreamed it, and now woke, half remembering what it was he dreamed. Would he ever again see Rouen, with its jumbled streets of crooked-timbered houses, the noisy, smelly fish markets he had played in as a child, or the ancient façade of Saint Ouen, its gable carved with the images of Judean kings and queens? An illimitable ocean separated him from that place, from that time; vertiginous walls of seas into which ships tumbled like paper boats. Was that other life a dream? Or was this a dream, this barbarous present in which he crouched in a hole beneath a tree trunk, alone, vulnerable as a lynx to an arrow in his throat?

Again, he crawled toward the opening and lifted his head into the light. He looked along the hidden path up which the Savages had dragged the lynx. He looked at the trees, high above the river. They are up there, hiding. They have lit no fire. They watch the trail and the river. Laforgue looked back at the river, curling into a bend. All was still. And then, closer, near the place where the Algonkin had landed yesterday, he saw two canoes drawn up on the riverbank. Coming up from them were Chomina, his wife and their little boy. Behind, his musket at the ready, as though to guard them, was Daniel. And lastly, the girl, Chomina's daughter. All of them looked around, looking for him.

At once Laforgue reached up from his hiding place and pulled himself to his feet. As he did, an eerie high-pitched yell struck into the silence. Ahead, he saw Chomina's party stop as if shot. Arrows hissed, some falling short, three finding a mark, one in Chomina's shoulder, one in his wife's neck, one in the bundle which his daughter carried on her back. At that moment Daniel's musket thundered. Seven painted Savages rushed out onto the trail, surrounding their victims, flailing at them with clubs. Laforgue saw Chomina turn to his wife as she fell, blood spurting from the arrow wound in her throat, saw Daniel on his knees, trying to protect his head and neck as the Savages with wild shrieks battered him down, saw the girl running with her little brother toward the canoes, saw four other Savages rush from the trees, pinioning her and tripping the child.

Laforgue stood, heart pounding. They had not seen him. Daniel's shot had felled one of the Savages, and now the Savage leader, wearing the mass vestments which he had donned last night, knelt by the fallen warrior, cradled him in his arms, then, with a cry of rage so terrible it made Laforgue quail, let the dead man fall back on the ground.

Rising, his silken robes bloodied from the dead man's wound, the Savage leader screamed to the others. Chomina's wife was dragged across the ground by one of her captors, while another ripped the arrow out of her neck. Laforgue saw them kick her and turn her over. The Savage leader, the embroidered gold cross on his vestments fouled with blood and dirt, uttered a second cry of rage, and at once the Savages fell on Chomina, Daniel and the girl, making them pass down a double line of warriors, each of whom struck at them with javelin or club. When Daniel, staggering, came in reach of the leader, the leader took a javelin, pulled Daniel's head back by his hair, then caught hold of Daniel's arm and held it up. With the point of his javelin he pierced Daniel's palm, laughing as the boy screamed in pain. Chomina, stumbling, fell to the ground. The Savages raised him up again, the better to beat him unconscious. The girl they punished with the staves of their javelins until they drew blood from her back and thighs. The little boy was the only member of the party they did not harm, one of them holding him by the hair as the child saw his mother bleeding from her dreadful arrow wound, his father bludgeoned senseless, his sister flayed. Again, the leader, brandishing Daniel's musket above his head, screamed an order. The Savages began to pass thongs over their captives' bodies, binding them, preparing to lead them to the canoes.

And in that moment, watching, Laforgue knew that Daniel, Chomina and Chomina's family all would die. And that he, if he crawled back into his hiding place, would escape their fate. But what is my life in the balance, if, by going forward now, I can confess Daniel, who is in a state of mortal sin, and, God willing, baptize the others before their last end?

He felt himself tremble. Deliberately slow, he began to walk toward the clearing. The painted Savages turned, their javelins poised, two of them threading their bows with arrows as he came toward the captives. The painted faces watched, impassive, as, pale and determined, a frail man in a long black robe, he knelt beside Chomina's wife and, wetting his fingers in the snow, began to say the words of baptism. He was too late. Tears came to his eyes as he saw her glazed pupils gaze past him at those heavens now forever denied her. Then, with a shriek of rage, the Savage leader came up behind him and clubbed him at the base of his skull. He fell forward, unconscious, and woke to hands passing thongs over his limbs. Within minutes, clubbed and bound, he stood with the others awaiting his fate.

The Savage strangers, silent now, loaded Laforgue's canoe with the remainder of the goods which Daniel earlier had strewn in the snow. Four warriors, coming from the trees, carried two canoes which Laforgue had not seen before, the canoes of the strangers. Within a minute all five canoes were launched in the waters of the lower rapids. With curses the painted Savages disposed of their captives, putting Daniel and Laforgue in one canoe and Chomina, his daughter and little son in the other. Then, with the Savage leader lifting his wet vestments up around his hips as he clambered aboard, and a second Savage, wearing Laforgue's spare cassock, pushing the leader's canoe to the front position, the strangers set out downriver. A light rain began to fall. Wincing, nursing his pierced hand, Daniel looked at Laforgue.

"We were coming back for you," he said.

"I know." Laforgue felt dizzy. The blow at the base of his skull had raised a large protrusion. "Your hand," he asked the boy. "Did they break the bones?"

"No, I don't think so."

"Chak, chak, chak, chak," said one of the painted faces, mimicking the French speech. Turning, he spat in Laforgue's face. "What is that dog talk, you hairy pig? What are you saying?"

"It is our tongue, the Norman tongue," Laforgue said. Again, pain stabbed at the base of his skull.

"We speak your tongue," Daniel said to the Savage. "What people are you? You speak like Hurons."

"Shut your hairy mouth," the Savage said. "If you cannot speak properly, then be silent, you prick."

The Savage then called to the two others who paddled at the rear of the canoe. "How is it that Normans can speak our tongue?"

"They talk like moose," one of the Savages said, laughing. "Algonkian moose. They will never sound like Iroquois."

"Fucking right."

Iroquois. Daniel looked at Laforgue. It was the danger Champlain had warned of. It was a sentence of death. Laforgue watched as Daniel, wincing, tried to lick his wounded hand. He leaned toward him. "Let me confess you," he whispered. "Say an act of contrition."

"Shut your fucking face," the Savage shouted, turning, striking Laforgue across the nose, making his nose bleed.

"Say the words to yourself," Laforgue whispered. "Not aloud."

Blood ran down his upper lip into his beard and mouth as he watched the boy close his eyes, watched his lips move in silent prayer. He felt a surge of joy. After a moment, Daniel opened his eyes, looked at him and nodded, as though to say he had finished. "*Ego te absolvo,*" Laforgue whispered, raising his hand in the sign of absolution. "*In nomine patris, et filii, et spiritus sancti.*"

The Savage who had struck him did not look back, for the canoes were now skimming at speed over rocky shallows, moving closer to shore. Laforgue, blood spilling down his chin onto his neck, nodded to Daniel to show that he had finished.

"Thank you," the boy whispered. "Forgive me, Father."

"God is with us," Laforgue said. "It is He who forgives us."

▼

After paddling less than an hour, the Savages abruptly swung back toward shore, landing a few leagues downriver from the place where the Algonkin had first made camp. Here they hid the canoes and their contents high in the trees, then roped together their prisoners. Shouting, cursing, beating them with javelin staves, they set off along a narrow track through the forest. Within minutes, Laforgue and Daniel heard cries ahead. Four Savage women came through the trees wearing necklaces of beads, their bodies naked to the waist as for a ceremonial feast. They carried bark platters containing strips of cooked meat which they gave to the returning warriors. Gleeful, they danced around the prisoners, pulling at Laforgue's beard, striking Annuka, her father and Daniel, calling out, "Let us caress them, let us caress them."

"Later," said the Savage leader, wolfing his meat and gesturing to the others to hasten on. And so, stumbling, bound, burdened, Chomina, his daughter and son, followed by Daniel and Laforgue, were led into an Iroquois village. Here were habitations of a sort Laforgue had never seen, dwellings laid out in a double row as in a village street with, at the end, a larger building, a communal house more than one hundred feet in length, built of strong saplings bent together to form an arched roof and covered with bark of oak and spruce. At the top of the arch was an open space to admit light and release the smoke of the fires.

As the warriors led their captives to this building, the party was surrounded by a large throng of men, women and children, all chanting at the tops of their voices. In the din Laforgue heard the beating of skin drums. At the entrance of the longhouse, a group of men, obviously leaders, stood waiting. They, like the warriors, had painted their faces. A few were heavily tattooed, their faces, backs and arms grotesquely traced in intricate arabesques. One of these tattooed figures, tall and gaunt, was adorned in such a profusion of colored shells and beads, and wore a beaver coat of such splendor, that Laforgue assumed him to be the paramount leader. It was to this man that the warriors led their prisoners.

"Normans," said the paramount chief.

"Traveling with Algonkin," said the leader of the hunters. He held out Daniel's musket. "Tarcha died of this."

The paramount leader took the musket eagerly, examined it, then pulled the trigger. There was no explosion. He shook it in vexation, then looked at Laforgue. "Bring them inside," he said to the hunters.

"Yes, Kiotsaeton."

The singing and drumming ceased. In a strange silence, the captives were led into the smoke-filled longhouse. Fires burned on the ground. Laforgue, looking up, saw rows of poles just under the vaulted roof. On them were suspended weapons, clothing, ornaments and skins. On a middle level were platforms running the length of the room and, as the captives were led to the fires, the villagers followed, scrambling up on these platforms to watch the spectacle.

"Strip them," said Kiotsaeton.

At once, all the prisoners, including the little boy, were stripped naked. A cheer went up into the rafters as the older women came forward, singing. They took firebrands from the smoking fire and approached the paramount chief.

"May we caress the captives?" asked one of the women.

"Caress them," said Kiotsaeton, "but carefully. We must make them last."

The women, gleeful, at once thrust their burning brands against the genitals of Chomina and Laforgue, causing them to double up in pain. They then burned Annuka's shoulder and thrust a flaming stick into Daniel's armpit. The crowd, wildly excited, yelled and shouted. "Make them sing, make them sing their songs."

"Sing," commanded Kiotsaeton. "Sing your war songs. And dance, you hairy dogs."

Savage hands pulled the two Frenchmen forward and amid kicks and shoves they were forced to perform a clumsy dance. "Sing," Daniel cried to Laforgue. "Sing or they will kill us."

"*Ave Maria,*" Laforgue sang hoarsely, the words of the hymn lost in the yells of the exultant Iroquois, "*gratia plena, Dominus tecum . . .*"

He looked and saw Daniel singing the hymn, his good hand clutching his armpit where he had been burned. Men and women now scrambled down from the platform and, going to the fires, took up hot coals on platters. These they sprinkled on the captives, all the while laughing and yelling in excitement. Then, as the captives writhed and shrank from these tortures, the leader issued a new command. At once all were silent.

He pointed to Chomina. "Sing. Sing your war song." He pointed to Annuka. "Dance."

Impassive, not looking at his captors, Chomina began to sing a war chant in a loud defiant voice. His daughter shuffled in a circle in a primitive dance step. Laforgue stared at the girl, his eyes misted by pain. That slender body which had aroused his lust now filled him with an infinite pity as her shoulders and narrow loins were kicked and pummeled by bystanders each time she stumbled and fell. *O Lord,* he prayed. *Grant me the chance to baptize her. Grant her eternal peace.*

And then, suddenly, the girl collapsed on the ground. The Savages fell silent; the only sound in the longhouse was Chomina's loud, monotonous war chant. Kiotsaeton and two other leaders went to the fires and spoke among themselves, then signaled to the waiting warriors. At once, a tall Savage, his head dyed red, his eyes horrid yellow circles, a strip of reddish fur hanging from a pigtail down his back, went up to Chomina's little boy, took him by the hair and, with a gesture callous as though he killed a fowl, swiftly slit his throat. Blood gurgled forth from the child's mouth. Daniel, anguished, tried to go toward him, but a Savage tripped him, spilling him on the ground. Chomina looked not at his dying son but up at the ceiling of the longhouse, singing a war chant as though he had seen nothing. And then, to his horror, Laforgue saw the child hacked to pieces with hatchets, its bloodied limbs thrown into a cooking kettle. He closed his eyes, as though unable to believe what he had witnessed.

Pandemonium filled the longhouse, a stamping, yelling, screaming din. The leader raised his hands for silence, then came up to Laforgue.

"Agnonha, who is Agnonha?"

"He is our leader, the leader of the French," Laforgue replied.

"Then you are a dead man, you hairy fool. Agnonha is the cunt who killed our people. You will die, but not today. You will die slowly. We will caress you and caress you again. Today, we will give you a first caress. Take his hand."

Two of the warriors at once seized and held Laforgue. Kiotsaeton took from his belt a razor-sharp clam shell. Taking Laforgue's left hand he pulled on the index finger; then, using the clam shell like a saw, cut to the bone. He sawed through the bone and pulled the skin and gristle free. He held up the finger joint. The crowd roared and cheered. He threw the piece of finger into the cooking kettle. In excruciating pain, Laforgue fell to his knees and then, in a scene so terrible that it surpassed horror or pity or forgiveness or rage, he saw three older women take from the cooking kettle the limbs of the dead child and pass them, parboiled, to the warriors who had captured Chomina's party. The warriors paraded up and down before Chomina and his daughter, eating the flesh as though it were succulent meat. Chomina stood, singing loudly, his eyes on the rafters. The girl vomited on the ground.

The women standing by the pot began to pass out parboiled flesh to other warriors. As they did, Kiotsaeton stepped forward and held up his arms. At once, the yelling died down.

"The prisoners must not die," Kiotsaeton shouted. "We will caress them again when the sun has risen. Give them food. Let the children caress them, but be careful. Give back their garments."

Surrounded by smiling, jeering Savages, the captives were thrown their clothes, forced to dress, then pushed and pulled outside the longhouse. Children danced ahead of them as they were led to a smaller dwelling where a fire burned on a pit of live coals. There, the villagers left them alone, save for one warrior with club and hatchet and four young and gleeful children. Exhausted, the captives lay down on the bare earth. The children circled them. One little girl giggled, her hand over her mouth, almost in a parody of embarrassment. "Take off your clothes," she said.

"Which ones?" the guard asked.

"Those two. The hairy ones."

"Take your fucking clothes off. Quick." The guard, raising his club, gave Laforgue and Daniel each a blow on the shoulder. Wearily, both men removed their garments and stood naked once again.

"Dance," cried a little boy. His companions, meanwhile, had gone to the rear of the habitation and returned now with sharpened sticks which they thrust into the flesh of the men's thighs.

Wearily, the captives began a shuffling dance.

"Sing," cried one child.

They began the Ave Maria.

"Be quiet," cried a second child.

They stopped singing. The first child, the one who had ordered them to sing, at once went to the fire and, picking up a burning brand, held it close to Daniel's penis. "I told you to sing," the child yelled.

Daniel began to sing.

"Stop!" cried the second child, approaching, also waving a burning brand. The guard laughed.

The little girl went up to Laforgue and pulled hard

on his beard. "What is this fucking shit on your face?" she cried. "Are you a man or a hare?"

"All right, children," the guard said indulgently. "That's enough. We must let them rest. There will be more sport tomorrow. Now they must eat."

"We will eat them," cried a little boy.

"I will eat your foot," the little girl screamed, dropping a hot coal on Daniel's foot.

"And I will eat one of your hands," a second boy yelled.

"Now, children, now, children," said the guard, laughing. "Outside, go on."

Yelling, giggling, the children ran out of the habitation. The two men, awkwardly, again put on their clothes. The guard bound their hands behind their backs, bound their feet so that they could only shuffle in a hobbled step. He bound Chomina and Annuka in a similar fashion, pausing to put his hand under the girl's skirt and fondle her. Then he brought pieces of some corn biscuit.

"Eat," he said to the girl and gently held the biscuit to her lips. Like an automaton, the girl tried to chew, but vomited the biscuit on the floor. "Never mind," the guard said quietly. "Later I will give you another piece."

He then went to Chomina, who bit on the biscuit he offered as though he did not see him. The guard fed Laforgue and Daniel, then went back to the fire, where, squatting on his hunkers, he took out his pipe and began to smoke.

For the first time since the capture, Chomina seemed to rouse himself. He shuffled close to his daughter, and she laid her head in his lap. He sat, rocking, rocking. Daniel hobbled across the floor and lay at her feet, looking at her with agonized tenderness. At last, her sobbing and retching ceased and she said to her father, "These aren't men. They're wolves."

"No," Chomina said. "They are not wolves. They are men. They are afraid of each other."

Laforgue, lying on the floor, turned to listen. "What do you mean?" he asked.

"If an Iroquois sees another Iroquois show pity to a captive, he will make fun of him. The warrior must not show pity. Pity is a weakness."

"They are wolves," the girl said again.

"No, no." Chomina looked down at her. "Our people do the same if they capture enemies. So do the Montagnais and the Huron. An enemy must be made to cry out in pain. That is why they torture us. But, alone, the Iroquois is like you or me." He nodded to the guard, who sat, his back to them, puffing on his pipe. "He will not harm us."

"Will we die?" she asked.

Her father rocked her but did not reply.

"But why must we cry out?" Daniel whispered. "Why?"

"If they can make us cry out, it means we cannot resist them. If we do not weep and plead for mercy, it means that when we die misfortunes will come upon them."

"But if we do cry out," Laforgue said. "Does that mean that they stop the torture?"

Chomina looked at him. "Don't you understand? If you cry out, then, when you die, they will possess your spirit."

"But that's not true," Laforgue said. "If I die, I will go to paradise. You and your daughter will come with me to paradise if you let me baptize you. I can do it now."

"Is that the water sorcery?"

"Yes. And all my God asks of you is that you believe in Him."

"Leave me alone," Chomina said bitterly. "I saw you do the water sorcery to my wife. But she was dead when you did it. She could not believe in your god, because she had died already. And some nights ago you did it to a baby. But the baby was dead. The water sorcery will not bring me to paradise. The water sorcery kills."

"You are wrong," Laforgue said. "Chomina, I am not lying to you. I will always be grateful to you. I can never repay you for coming back. But if you let me baptize you I swear that when you die you will go to paradise."

"What paradise? A paradise for Normans?"

"No. For you. For all who are baptized."

"But my people are not baptized with this water sorcery. Therefore they are not in your paradise. Why would I want to go to a paradise where there are none of my people? No, I will die and go to another country where our dead have gone. There I will meet my wife and my son. Your God shits on me and mine. My wife is dead because of you. My son is in the stomachs of the Iroquois. And the Iroquois will kill me slowly, day after day. It is you Normans, not the Iroquois, who have destroyed me, you with your greed, you who do not share what you have, who offer presents of muskets and cloth and knives and kettles to make us greedy as you are. And I have become as you, greedy for things. And that is why I am here and why we will die together."

"You are right about our greed," Laforgue said. "But you are wrong about our God."

"Leave him," Daniel whispered. "Be quiet, Father."

And so they lay in the smoking habitation, silent, in pain, each alone in thought of what had happened that day and what lay ahead. In the opening of the roof, the sky darkened to night. And when, at last, Chomina saw that their guard was asleep, he began to whisper to his daughter. Daniel, licking the wound in his palm, heard their muted voices and crawled closer to listen. But as he did, Chomina turned and looked at him in the flames of the guttering fire, as though warning him to stay away.

It was much later when, exhausted from their wounds and sufferings, both Chomina and Laforgue slept, that Annuka, inching herself across the bare earth, came and lay, bound, against her bound lover. In the darkness, he could not see her face. "Annuka," he whispered. "Your father is right. I have destroyed you."

Her face came close. He felt her parched lips touch his cheek.

▼

At sunset, in the long room, tobacco was handed around. The seven in council moved to the central fire, some lying down, some squatting on their haunches. Pipes were lit. In the background, dogs barked and children cried, but on the sleeping trestles above the council, men and women turned away, showing by their posture that they respected their leaders' need for private debate. Kiotsaeton, who had called the meeting, listened first to Agariata and then to Honatheniate. Both were council chiefs but not leaders in war. Both were skilled in argument and memory. Both spoke at length. By the time Honatheniate had finished, the council had smoked two pipes. Pulling his beaver robe open, for it was warm in the long room, Kiotsaeton spoke at last. First he made a summary of the arguments he had listened to, for this was the custom and proved that one had heard and understood. He made no judgments on the arguments. When he had finished, he asked merely, "Is this what all have heard?"

The council made sounds of assent.

"Then let me give you a different solution," Kiotsaeton said. "About the girl, there is no question that, as Agariata has said, she is the only female captive and, as such, must be offered as a gift to Areskoui, by burning at the stake. Are all agreed?"

All were agreed.

"As for her fucking dog of a father, we will not let him defy us. We will caress him day and night until he screams like a hare. We will cut strips of skin from his body, we will burn him with coals and remove his fingers one by one, until he can no longer protect or feed himself."

"Even so, he will not be easy," said one of the council. "I watched him. He did not even look at his fucking child as the warriors ate it."

"He is a stupid Algonkian prick," Kiotsaeton said. "We will bring Ontitarac to work on him. Ontitarac will make him scream and give us his spirit. Eh, Ontitarac?"

Ontitarac, old, tattooed from head to navel, opened his robe and pulled on his penis, grinning at the others. Everyone laughed.

"Now we come to the Normans," Kiotsaeton said. "And this is serious business. Do you know what those Normans mean to us? Especially the Blackrobe? Do you know what Agnonha will say in Québec when he hears that we have killed them?"

"I don't give a shit what Agnonha will say," said Agariata.

"Remember. The Blackrobe is a sorcerer," said Kiotsaeton.

"We are not afraid of any sorcerers, even a Blackrobe," said old Ontitarac defensively. "That is why I say caress them unto death. Both have already cried out. They are weak. When they die we will eat their hearts and own their powers."

Kiotsaeton spat onto the fire. It was his way of signaling that now he would tell what was really in his mind. The others were silent. "Two Normans are twenty muskets," he told the council.

"Twenty muskets?"

"From Agnonha."

"Agnonha," said Honatheniate, "that cunt, that hairy dog. Our enemy will die in shit before I trade with him."

"Twenty," said Kiotsaeton.

"The muskets kill only once," said a council member.

"No, they can kill many times," said Kiotsaeton. "The Normans kill with them, again and again. It is a thing that must be learned, like the bow and arrow."

"He is right," said Annentaes, who was a war chief and rarely spoke.

"Twenty muskets," said Kiotsaeton. "And I would

also ask for ten French kettles, thirty of their steel knives and some wampum belts."

"Ask what you want," said Ontitarac. "I tell you what Agnonha will give. He will give death and vengeance from generation to generation. That is what that fuckpot will give. When the Mohawk killed a Norman, Agnonha sent his warriors with arquebuses to destroy their villages. He will not trade with them or treat with them now, eight winters after the death."

"Exactly," said Kiotsaeton. "Let me say that I, like Ontitarac, do not fear any Norman. Not even that fucker Agnonha. But twenty muskets. Twenty muskets. Think of it, you men."

"Wait," said Manitougache. "Why should the Normans give guns to us, their enemies? They do not like to give guns to any of the people, not even to the Algonkin who are their allies."

"True," said Agariata. "The Normans are not like the Dutchmen. Agnonha refused to trade, even when the Montagnais offered him fifty beaver peltries for each musket."

"He cannot let a Norman die," said Kiotsaeton. "Especially a Blackrobe. It is said the Blackrobes hold him in their power."

"The Blackrobes are the worst of sorcerers," said old Ontitarac. "I have heard they live in a separate habitation, always. When they live among the Huron they will not allow the Huron to sleep in their dwellings. In each of the Blackrobe habitations there is a special room. In that room, there is a small box placed on a high ledge. Inside the box there are pieces of a corpse which they brought from France. They say this corpse is the body of their god. They have secret ceremonies in which they eat little pieces of this fucking corpse."

"That is true," said another council member. "I have been told the same story. And by a Huron."

"I have heard another thing," said Honatheniate. "It is that the Blackrobes do not fuck. They never fuck. They do not fuck because it increases their powers as sorcerers."

There was an uneasy silence. "Well," said Kiotsaeton, "that proves what I said. Agnonha fears the Blackrobe sorcerers. He will not dare to let one die in our hands."

"You are right," said old Ontitarac. "He kisses their asses and fears their spells. I have heard the same story up and down the river many winters now."

"Twenty muskets and the other goods," Kiotsaeton said, and smiled at the council. "We will not have to bargain. We have all power on our side."

"But how can we get the muskets?" asked Honatheniate. "We would go to give up the Normans and walk into an ambush. You cannot deal with a fucking Norman leader like Agnonha. He is a liar and has always been one. He does not keep his word."

"We will deal through the Dutchmen who live on the farther shore," Kiotsaeton said. "We will send a messenger to their place and tell them to tell the Normans that we have two of their men. When the guns are given to the Dutchmen, we will give them the prisoners."

"I see a trap," said Agariata.

"It will be a trap that can kill only one of us," Kiotsaeton said. "One man can bring the two prisoners to the place of the Dutchmen. If the muskets are there, he will give them the prisoners. If not, or if there is some trap, he will kill the prisoners."

"And which man will volunteer to go into that fucking mess?" asked Agariata, smiling.

Kiotsaeton spat in the fire. "I am the man."

▼

When the light in the roof opening of the prisoners' habitation signaled that a new day had begun, Chomina, still feigning sleep, rolled over and made a covert signal to his daughter. The guard had wakened and was lying by the embers of the fire, eating a piece of the corn biscuit left over from the night before. Chomina watched as Annuka got up and hobbled painfully to where the guard lay. Chomina spoke to the wolf, his reigning spirit. She must not fail. For if she fails, by tonight the Iroquois will have caressed me to a point where I can no longer use my hands. I still have my hands, Chomina told the wolf. With my hands I can be free. Still pretending sleep, he rolled over and looked at the Normans. Both lay as though in dreams, although the boy moaned from time to time.

Annuka, obeying her father, came up to the guard very slowly, head bent in a posture which offered him no threat.

"I want to shit," she said, in a low voice.

The guard smiled and chewed on his biscuit. "Well, shit, then," he said. "Go over there. I don't want you to shit over me."

She held out her bound hands. "The cords are so tight," she said, "My hands are like the hands of a dead man. When I try to get down to shit, my ankles fail and I fall on my face. Help me."

He laughed. "Help you? I cannot shit for you, you silly cunt."

Tears came into her eyes. In her pain and fear it was not difficult for her to make tears. The guard was young. They are men, not wolves, her father had said. If no one sees him, he will not be afraid that he will be mocked. If no one sees him, he may show you mercy. Her father was right.

"Come here, pretty," the guard said. She came up close to him in tiny steps, her ankles chafing from the hobble. She felt his hands on her numbed wrists. Her bonds were loosened. "Go on," he said. "Do it there."

She hobbled to the place he had pointed out. As she went there, she flexed her numbed fingers and moved her wrists. She raised her skirt and showed him her bum. She knew he was watching her. She let him look at it; then, pretending she had finished, she hobbled back to him, smiling to show her gratitude.

He was sitting up now, and she saw to her excitement that he had loosened his clothes around his thighs and taken out a large stiff prick. He looked up at her, grinning. "Lie down, pretty," he said. "Wait." He came to her and knelt at her feet. "I cannot fuck you with your legs tied together," he whispered. He looked back at the Normans and at her father. All three seemed to sleep.

She felt herself tremble as though she would faint. He freed her ankles and, numbed, she fell on her knees. "It hurts," she said. "It was so tight."

The guard smiled. He massaged her ankles, then

fondled her breasts. He signaled her to kneel so that he could put it in from behind.

"Wait," she said. "I am hungry. Can I first have a bite?"

That was something he understood. He grinned at her; then, still with a stiff prick sticking up against his belly, went to the platter and bent down to get the corn biscuit. As he turned his back she reached for the heavy club. It was so heavy, for a moment she thought she could not lift it above her head. But she remembered the warriors standing by the kettles as they wolfed Outiji's flesh. She whirled the club. He turned, quick as a deer, but as he did she smashed the heavy club full in his face, knocking him back into the dying fire. You must make sure, her father had said. If you have a chance, you must make sure, and at once. So she ran forward and, choking, sick, raised the heavy club again and battered his head until it was a pulp of blood and matted hair. She dropped the club. He made little noise. She vomited into the embers.

The Normans were awake, lying on their sides, as was her father, all of them watching her. "Quick," her father said. He had told her to untie him first.

She went to him, but as she passed Iwanchou she looked into his eyes. She stopped, bent over him and began to free his bonds.

"Annuka," her father called in a low, angry voice. "Stop that. Don't touch him. Come to me."

She looked back at her father. "We cannot leave them," she said.

"The Iroquois want them more than they want us," her father said. "And besides, he has an injured hand. Leave him alone."

"No," she said. She freed Iwanchou's hands, and he began to undo the cords which bound his feet. She went to her father and freed him. He was angry at her disobedience, but when his bonds were removed he stood and embraced her. Iwanchou was untying the Blackrobe. "All right," her father said. "Nicanis, conceal your robe under the clothes of the dead one. Remember, we too are dead men if we are discovered. How many *raquettes* are there here?"

In addition to the snowshoes of the dead guard, they found several other pairs, stored on shelves which hung down from the roof. There were also heavy winter garments of moose hide which they used as cloaks. Chomina took the dead guard's knife and handed the hatchet to Laforgue and the club to Daniel. Then, with snowshoes tied to his back and his head muffled in skins, he went to the opening of the habitation. "Wait," he said. He went out and in less than a minute was back. "The Iroquois sleep late. There is no snow, and we are minutes from the river. Cover your hairy faces and be quick."

Outside, the village had not yet wakened. A few dogs wandered in the street, searching for scraps of food. Smoke from dying fires came from the roofs of the dwellings, and in the distance, at the end of the village, could be seen tilled fields, now cleared of their autumnal harvest. Chomina looked up toward the council longhouse where three women squatted by the doorway, picking and eating each other's lice. The women did not see them. "Walk slowly," Chomina said. He took the arm of Laforgue, who was unsteady on his feet. They walked down the village street, coming to the trail which led to the river. Yesterday's snow had melted, leaving the ground wet and muddy. As they came to the last of the dwellings, they saw, sitting on a heap of firewood, two little boys playing a game with a wooden ball tied to a string, which they threw up in the air and attempted to catch in an attached wooden cup. The children paid them no attention, but, as Daniel passed, he recognized one of the boys as the child who had tormented him the day before. He sunk his head in the rough cape of skin so that he could barely see the ground in front of him and, despite himself, quickened his pace. But the children, intent on their game, did not look up, and within a minute the village was out of sight as hurrying now, moving at a run, Chomina went ahead. The landing place by the river was unguarded. Circling restlessly among the Iroquois canoes, Chomina found his own and the one used by Laforgue. Hidden in the nearby trees were paddles, portage ropes and cooking kettles, which he placed in each of the two canoes. As he finished, his daughter reached the clearing, and when, a moment later, Laforgue and Daniel entered the area, they saw the two, father and daughter, in a whispered, angry discussion.

"Do what I say."

"No!"

"Come on." Chomina took her arm and dragged her toward his canoe. At that moment Daniel ran up beside them.

"What is this?"

"Shh!" Chomina glanced up the path leading to the Iroquois village. "We are going back to our people. You two get in the other canoe. Hurry. The Iroquois will soon be awake."

"I told you," Annuka said to her father. "I will go in Iwanchou's canoe. Let go of me."

Chomina released her arm and turned away as

though to leave. Suddenly, he turned back to face Daniel, and now, in his hand, was the guard's knife. "She's my daughter. She comes in my canoe."

"Do not listen to him," the girl said. "He plans to leave you both."

Chomina, with astonishing agility, leaped on Daniel, circling his neck with his arm, the knife which he held in his left hand laid across the boy's throat. Slowly, he turned Daniel around to face Annuka. "Get in my canoe. Now, or I will cut this Norman's throat."

The girl stared at him, then slowly, obeying, walked toward the river's edge. "Hurry!" her father said. "Do you want us to burn in their fires?"

All three had forgotten Laforgue, who moved up behind them quietly and pulled out the hatchet Chomina had given him. "Let go of him," he said. Chomina, caught by surprise, wheeled, turning to face Laforgue, and at that moment the boy broke Chomina's grip, tripping him, falling on him, his good hand closing on Chomina's knife arm. The priest, running up, stood over Chomina, menacing him with the hatchet. "Give me the knife!" Laforgue said.

Chomina, lying on his back, felt a sudden fear of this Blackrobe sorcerer who stood above him like a manitou, waiting to cleave his skull. He dropped the knife and the boy picked it up.

"No one is angry, Chomina," the priest said. "Now, let us all travel in one canoe."

"Where will we go?" Daniel asked.

"To our winter hunting place," Chomina said, scrambling to his feet. "But we must travel quickly. When they find us gone, they will guess where we went. It is the only place we can go now."

"No," said Laforgue. "We can go up the rapids."

"Nicanis is right," the girl said to her father. "They will not think of that. And the Iroquois of this place do not travel above the rapids."

Chomina, his eyes still on the path leading back to the village and danger, stood for a moment, undecided. Then he turned to his daughter. "Go with them. I will go south, alone."

"Come with us, Father. I am asking you."

Again, her father looked back at the path. "You leave me no fucking choice, do you?" he said. "If I let you go alone with these hairy fools, you are a dead woman, even if the Iroquois do not come upon you. All right. We will go up the rapids. But in two canoes. You and Iwanchou in one, Nicanis and I in the other."

"Right," Daniel said, and smiled. "Then we know that you will follow us."

"Come on," Chomina said. "Hurry." But as he went to the canoes, he paused and looked at his daughter. "Remember, if I am killed today, I am not angry with you. They have put a spell on you, these Normans. You are not to blame."

"You will not be killed," she said. "Look." She pointed to the sky. A file of geese flew in a straight line, passing overhead with a rush of wings. "They go north," she said. "It is a sign."

Chomina leaped into the first canoe, led them out into the ebb of the main current, then turned north. Peering ahead as he paddled, he said to Laforgue, "You are not so stupid as you look, Nicanis. But remember, there may be other Iroquois fuckers waiting for us near the rapids. We are still dead men."

In less than an hour they again reached the rushing

currents which signaled the beginning of the rapids. They passed the scene of their capture. Several hundred yards farther on, the rapids became foaming white shallows. The canoes stalled. Chomina, wading in the water, tied portage ropes, and soon all four were in the rapids, hauling the canoes over slippery rocks, sometimes falling and bruising their knees, sometimes forced to carry the canoes and climb narrow trails beside the falls. No one spoke. Their bodies ached not only from toil but from the wounds and beatings inflicted on them, yet all the while they moved in a heightened, anxious state, waiting for the hiss of a stone-headed arrow or the killing cry of the enemy.

Here, at the falls, there was no snow on the ground. The weather in this limbo of seasons had vacillated back to a strange warmth, and soon, in their heavy winter clothing, the priest and Daniel were dripping with sweat. They toiled on until early evening, when suddenly Chomina recognized something. He beckoned and, carrying the canoes, they came into a place where the river widened into a great pool below a thunder of falls. Chomina put the canoes back in the water and skillfully navigated the falls, leading them into a sheltered place beneath the roaring waters. There, he disembarked and beached the canoes on a grassy knoll.

"Wait here," he said. They saw him crawl across some green-slimed rocks and reach down into a hole. A few minutes later, he came back with some pieces of dried eel and husks of corn. "Hurons went up this way and have not come back down," he said. "This is one of their caches. If we can find the others, we will have food for the next three nights. They picked this place because there is no need to build a shelter. It is warm here, under the waters."

In the roar of the falls, sustained talk was impossible. Weary, aching, spent, they ate their small meal and curled up beside each other, covering themselves with skins and bark. Before they slept, Laforgue washed and cleaned the pus and dirt which had accumulated in Daniel's pierced hand. All were in pain, the girl from the beating and the lacerations on her thighs, Chomina from the arrow wound in his back and the heavy blows which had raised ugly weals on his neck and shoulder, Laforgue from genital burns and the severed joint on his index finger.

Before lying down, Laforgue thought to read his breviary but realized that for the first time in his life as a priest this was no longer possible. Sewn into his cassock were the only possessions left to him, his rosary, the map, and Father Bourque's instructions. His breviary, like all else—mass vestments, missals, the sacred communion vessels—had been lost forever. Into his mind came a vision of the Iroquois leader, rising up, clad in sacrilege in silken white and gold, the embroidered gold cross on his breast bloodied and stained with dirt. Again, in the light of the cooking fires, he saw the warriors gleeful as devils, their white teeth tearing the parboiled flesh of Chomina's child.

He looked at Chomina. The Savage lay on his side, his cloak drawn up around his neck. His eyes, obsidian, opaque, were fixed on the rushing falls; his bruised and blood-clotted face was impassive as a head carved in stone. Less than twenty-four hours ago, this Savage had a wife, a son and an honored place among his people.

Now he had seen both die barbarous deaths, had watched his daughter batter in a man's skull and was, with her, fugitive in a wilderness where, at any moment, cannibal enemies might again attack. What is he thinking, Laforgue wondered, this man who lives his life in outer darkness, far from the sight of God? What consolation can he seek, he who knows nothing of God's mercy? And Daniel. What is in *his* mind tonight, he who has come so sudden to man's estate and to this nightmare vision of a world few men ever see?

Laforgue looked at the girl, who lay, her head nestled against Daniel's chest, her eyes closed, her face shut in as though she were a mystic deep in prayer. Yet she knew nothing of prayer; she, like her father, was far from the sight of God, knowing nothing of God's mercy.

But as these thoughts jumbled in Laforgue's mind, the word *mercy, mercy, mercy*, repeated itself like a meaningless stammer in his brain. What mercy? If Our Lord tests me, if He tests Daniel, then He promises us something which repays us a thousandfold for any suffering, any danger, any death. But what does He offer to these others, what mercy does He show to these Savages who will never look on His face in paradise, these He has cast into outer darkness, in this land which is the donjon of the devil and all his kind?

9

To reach the upper river beyond the rapids, they traveled three days. Most of that time they spent inland, away from the water, carrying their canoes as they trudged along a path worn by countless Savage travelers, a path which climbed a steep hill and brought them to a view in which the Ottawa River stretched clear ahead. In those three days and nights Chomina barely broke silence. He seemed to come to life only when, each evening, he searched for caches in which other travelers had stored food. Gradually, the silence which enveloped him spread to the others as they toiled on from dawn to dusk, up steep inclines, through bush and bracken, their wounds now part of a generalized torment which, in a mixture of fatigue and pain, seemed to anesthetize them and force them on.

Laforgue brooded endlessly on the journey ahead. Without proper weapons to hunt game, without supplies of food or goods to trade with the Allumette nation which they would shortly encounter, without even a guide should Chomina decide to abandon them, he must somehow complete this dreadful journey. According to Father Bourque's instructions he was now some twelve days from his destination. He must travel north on the Ottawa and Mattawa for five days, then cross Lake Nipissing and find the smaller river which led to that great lake of which Father Brabant had written, "It is a great gentle sea of fresh water, so huge that no farther shore is ever in sight." He must travel south along the shores of this great lake until he reached the Ihonatiria mission. If it still existed. He no longer allowed himself the luxury of hope. He who all his life had put his trust in God now paddled silent behind a Savage, his mind empty of prayer. At night he lay down like an animal and slept without thought of his nightly devotions. It was as though in these last days of degradation, pain and horror, his mind had become numb to moral judgments. He saw Daniel lie in the arms of a Savage girl and felt no anger, no sense of sin. He moved, blind and uncaring, shut out from God's sight as though he, like Chomina, was condemned to live forever in the darkness of this land.

Three days after passing the head of the rapids, Chomina failed to find any further cache of food. Nothing was said. But on the morning of the fifth day, paddling, faint with hunger, suddenly Laforgue saw Chomina turn their canoe toward shore. Perhaps he had sighted hares or deer in the woods? As the canoe slipped into the shallows by the riverbank and Annuka and Daniel turned their craft to follow, Laforgue saw Chomina's face. The Savage, whose normal complexion was a brick red color, had now taken on a purplish hue. Suddenly, he leaned forward, his paddle trailing the water, his breathing hoarse and constricted. When they beached the canoe, he got out slowly and, shaking off Laforgue's helping arm, walked alone, up to the top of the bank.

"Are you ill?" Laforgue asked, but the Savage shook his head as though the question were an irrelevance. At the top of the bank he sat down heavily and gestured to Laforgue to sit beside him.

At that moment his daughter and Daniel came up, concerned. Chomina beckoned her to come close, then whispered something which Laforgue did not catch. At once, she took Daniel by the arm and walked him away. When they were out of earshot, Chomina, breathing heavily, looked at Laforgue. "Tell me, Nicanis. What does your dream say now?"

"I am too weary for dreams."

"But you *must* dream," Chomina said and clutched his chest as though in pain. "If you do not dream, how can you see the journey ahead?"

"I put my trust in God. He will decide what must happen to me."

For a long moment, Chomina said nothing. He squatted on the ground, his knees up, his head hanging down in a posture which recalled to Laforgue a madman he had seen in the days of his youth, squatting among the cluster of beggars outside the cathedral at Coutances, a figure so frightening in its dejection that Laforgue, coming from the church, would hurry past, eyes averted, his mind mumbling a prayer as though it were a spell to cast out the devil.

"Then your god has told you to go on?" Chomina said, at last.

"Yes."

"In two days you will be in the country of the Allumette. You will need their help. You have no food and nothing to give them in trade. How will you go on?"

"God will provide," Laforgue said, but the words were stones in his mouth.

"How? If he does not provide, my daughter will die. You, Nicanis, I understand. You Blackrobes welcome death. You think that, if you die, you will enter a Norman paradise. But if my daughter dies, she will go to the land of night."

"If she will accept our Lord," Laforgue began, but the Savage, breathing heavily and in pain, silenced him with a gesture.

"That is no answer," Chomina said. "How can we believe you? You have not seen this paradise of which you speak. I have not seen our world of night, but I know it is no paradise. You have no sense, Nicanis. No man should welcome death."

"You are wrong," Laforgue said. "For us, it is this world which is the world of night."

"What shit you speak. Look around you. The sun, the forest, the animals. This is all we have. It is because you Normans are deaf and blind that you think this world is a world of darkness and the world of the dead is a world of light. We who can hear the forest and the river's warnings, we who speak with the animals and the fish and respect their bones, we know that is not the truth. If you have come here to change us, you are stupid. We know the truth. This world is a cruel place but it is the sunlight. And I grieve now, for I am leaving it."

Laforgue glanced sharply at Chomina. As he did, the Savage bowed his head, withdrawing into that posture of frightening dejection which recalled the madman of Coutances. Some paces away, the girl and Daniel sat silent, watching. And, at that moment, Laforgue heard a chorus of birds announce the limits of their territories. If snow had fallen here, it had not lasted on the ground, and even now in the first days of November the trees were a last blaze of crimson and yellow leaves. The world is our sunlight, Chomina says, and for him it is true. I am not permitted to baptize him against his will. Laforgue looked at the Savage, ill, suffering, waiting for death. And, despairing, thought of God's mercy denied him. I must not dwell on these things. It is the devil who puts such thoughts in my head. But is it the devil? What has happened to me? Why do I no longer pray?

"Chomina," he said. "We will prepare a bed for you and we will rest here until you are stronger."

"I will not grow stronger," Chomina said. "I am ill. I will not see one more night. Send my daughter to me and I will speak with her. Then, all of you, get in the canoe and go on. At once."

"No, no, we will stay with you."

"Hairy fucking fool," Chomina said, with the ghost of his usual smile, "send Annuka to me."

▼

The Blackrobe was coming toward her. But she had already risen because the forest had warned her. And now as she walked across the ground that separated her from her father, she knew that the She Manitou waited in the trees. Trembling, she passed the trees and came to her father. Already, he had assumed the pose of those who live in the world of night, squatting, his head down, his arms folded across his chest. "Father," she said. He looked up; his eyes were glazed with a film of sickness. "Is it a wound?"

Her father shook his head. "This morning when I woke, blood was in my mouth. Also, I shit black and cannot stop it. It is over with me. When I paddled past this place, the She Manitou called."

"Have you seen Her?"

"No. But I will. And She will touch me before night comes."

She knelt beside him and put her hand on his shoulder. His body was like stone. "We will stay with you until then."

"No. I must be alone. I have dreamed this. As I brought the canoe into this place, it was as though I had come home. That rock there, that line of trees, even this mound where I sit, all of it has been in my dreams for many years. Often I have asked myself what this place means. But it is not granted to us to know what some dreams mean. If only I had known then that it was the dream of death. That I would die in a quiet place and alone. Think what a gift that would have been. I would have been brave. I would have been a great warrior."

"You are a great warrior," she said.

"No. I am stupid and greedy and blind as any Norman. Because of that my wife and son are dead and now you will be left alone here with these cripples."

"Iwanchou is my betrothed," she said. "He will not abandon me."

Her father bent over, coughed and spat blood on the ground. "There is one chance for you. For both of you. Leave the Blackrobe and go back to our people. You must travel at night. The Iroquois do not hunt at night. I told that to Neehatin, but he has no fucking sense. Iwanchou can learn how to use a bow. You can make a bow for him."

"His hand is injured," she said.

"The winter hunting place is only seven nights away. The Blackrobe must go on alone. That is Neehatin's dream for him."

"You said that Neehatin has no sense."

Her father ground his teeth in pain. "Do not argue with me! Do as I tell you."

"I will do it," she said.

"Good. Now, go and bring some pine branches. I want to lie down."

She did as he told her. She took the hunting knife and cut the branches. As she did, Iwanchou came to her. "Can I help?"

"No. Leave us."

She went back to her father. When she had arranged the branches in a pallet for him, he lay on them and looked up at the sky. The film over his eyes had thickened. Perhaps he no longer saw her. "Are you hungry?" she asked. "I can look for berries."

He shook his head. "Go. Put both canoes in the water. Let the Blackrobe travel alone in the second canoe. When you and Iwanchou reach the current, turn south. The Blackrobe is sick and paddles like a child. He will not be able to overtake you."

Tears burned her eyes. "I will stay with you," she said.

Slowly, her father turned his head and looked at her. "I lied to you," he said. "When I landed here, the She came from the woods and touched me. She is waiting. When we are alone, She will lead me quickly to the land of night."

Fear came upon her. It seemed to her that she heard the She Manitou crying in the trees.

"Go," her father said. She bent and embraced him. She wept.

"I weep too," her father said. "But I have no tears left."

She turned from him, then, and ran back to the place where the Normans waited. "Come," she told Iwanchou. "Launch the canoes. My father is dying. He must be alone."

"Can I speak with him?"

"No. We do not have farewells. Come with me."

But the Blackrobe, hearing this, at once rose and went over to her father. She hurried after him. "Come away," she said angrily.

"Chomina," said the Blackrobe, kneeling and joining his palms together. "Chomina, do you hear me? If you can hear me, please listen. My God loves you, as I do. If you will accept his love, he will admit you to paradise."

"Come away," she said. She pulled on the Blackrobe's hair, making him wince.

"Let me be," the Blackrobe said. "Let me at least say one prayer for him."

"You fucking sorcerer!" she screamed. "Leave him alone. Iwanchou? Help me!"

Iwanchou ran up.

"Take him away," she cried. "Let my father die in peace."

She heard them speak with each other in their tongue. Iwanchou then pushed and pulled the Blackrobe, moving him toward the place of the canoes. She looked at her father. He no longer saw her with the eyes of the land of day. He looked toward the trees and she knew that he was looking in the face of the terrible One. In fear, she ran back to the Normans. "Quick," she said to Iwanchou. "Get in the canoes. Hurry, Nicanis!"

But the Blackrobe, ignoring her, knelt down again, his hands clasped, staring at the sky, his lips moving in some sorcery. She slapped his face. "Come. We must not be here when he dies. Get in the canoe."

He rose and came with her. She screamed to them to hurry as they dragged the canoes down into the river. She and Iwanchou got into one, the Blackrobe into the other. Paddling in hurried strokes, she moved into the main current, the Blackrobe in his canoe following behind. When the canoes stood well offshore, she looked back. Her father lay alone in the clearing, resting on the pallet of branches. But, as she watched, his spirit rose out of his body. The spirit of her dead father walked toward the trees, his hand in the She Manitou's hand.

▼

The canoes stalled, riding the current. Daniel kept theirs moving in a circle so that Annuka could watch the shore. After a while, she turned to look at him. She said, "It is a rule with the Algonkin that no children shall lack parents. If I go back to them, they will give me a new family."

"I am your family," he told her.

"My father said we should go back to the winter hunting place. Come with me. Let Nicanis go on alone."

Daniel looked at the other canoe, at the priest who steered it. "I cannot leave him now."

Again she watched the shore. "I promised my father that I would go back. It is foretold in Neehatin's dream that Nicanis will enter a Huron village alone."

"Listen to me," Daniel said. "That dream cannot be fulfilled if we leave him. Look at him. How can we leave him?"

"That sorcerer, what do I care?" she said. "You saw him just now with my father."

"That was foolish, yes," Daniel said. "But he wanted to help him, not to harm him."

She looked over at the priest, then said, "We two could travel by night on the river. It is only seven nights' journey."

"I cannot leave him, Annuka."

He saw the glitter of anger in her eyes. "Then love him. Love that sorcerer and go with him, since you love him more than you love me."

"You know that's not true."

"I know you are a Norman. My father was right. The Blackrobe has you in his spell. All right, let's change canoes."

"Annuka . . ."

She took up her paddle. "We will land at the next bend of the river. We can't land here. The She Manitou is in those trees. But you, you fool, you're too blind to know that."

Suddenly, anger filled him like a drunkenness. "Father Laforgue," he called. "Follow us. We're going to change canoes."

Angry, he stroked, not bothering to match his stroke to hers. She thinks I'm stupid, but it is she who is stupid, a stupid Savage who will go back down there to torture, death, to cannibals! Because a stupid Savage like Neehatin had a dream. All right. Let her go.

A few minutes later they beached both canoes out of sight of Chomina's body. Laforgue saw the girl take a cooking kettle from her canoe and put it in his. "Good idea," he said. "It's better that we travel in one canoe."

"I told you he was stupid," she said, not looking at Daniel.

"No more stupid than someone who goes back down among cannibals."

"Be quiet," she said. "Your voice isn't a man's voice but the squealing of a hare."

"What's wrong?" Laforgue asked. "Annuka, Daniel, what's wrong?"

"You know very well what's wrong." She burst into tears. "You put a spell on him. He loved me and you took away that love. You hairy shit. I loved him. I love him."

"Daniel," Laforgue said, turning to the boy. "Listen, do you want to go back down the rapids?"

"No, I don't," Daniel said, and Laforgue saw that he

too was close to tears. I don't. But I . . . I can't—I don't want to leave her."

"Talk, talk, talk," the girl said, angry and weeping. "What are you jabbering about?"

"We cannot let her go back alone," the priest told Daniel. "She has lost her family because of us. What am I to do? If I send you with her and you lie with her and do not convert her and marry her, then you will destroy your soul."

"If that is what worries you," Daniel said, "I promise you I will try to convert her."

"Then go with her."

Daniel hesitated, then said to the girl, "He wants me to go with you."

She stopped weeping. "And you, what do you want?"

"I want to be your husband. I will live with your people."

"I warn you," she said. "They won't treat you well."

"Then come with me to the Hurons," Daniel said. "We can live there. And Nicanis will marry us."

"Is that true?" she asked Laforgue.

Daniel looked at Laforgue and said, in French, "Tell her yes."

Laforgue looked at the girl. "Yes, it is true," he said. "You can live among us as his wife."

She turned and walked back to the river. She stood, staring downriver at the bend behind which her father's body lay. At last she turned back. She looked at Daniel and then at Laforgue. "I have decided," she said. "Now I am your family. We will go in one canoe."

10

On the morning of November 10, Casson and Vallier, two fur traders returning from the Huron country, came down from the Upper Lake into the Mattawa River with six Algonkian paddlers and four canoes, heavily laden with furs. They were excited and nervous, for they were two weeks behind plan and racing the approaching snows. Ahead, in a bend of the river, they saw a solitary canoe approach, its occupants paddling in a desultory fashion. Casson could not make out the nature of these strangers. "Nipissing?" he asked, touching the shoulder of his lead paddler.

"Blackrobe," the paddler said.

Shit, Casson said to himself. He was a Huguenot. "One of your Fathers," he called back to Vallier.

"Shit," said Vallier. "Let's tell him we're in a hurry."

But Casson, uneasy now, stared ahead. Why only one canoe? The Jesuits usually traveled with several canoes, all filled with mission supplies. Had the other paddlers run away?

As his men stroked swiftly, closing the gap, Casson saw that there was one Jesuit, a French boy and a Savage girl in the canoe. He touched his lead paddler and pointed to the girl.

"Algonkian," the paddler said.

The Jesuit began to wave at them, asking them to pull in to shore. Casson looked back, questioning Vallier. Vallier shrugged.

"Hallo. Hallo," the Jesuit called in a hoarse voice. "We need help."

Unwillingly, Casson gave the order to land. At that point, coming close to the solitary canoe, he saw that all three occupants had been beaten and wounded. His spine prickled. He looked again at the Jesuit and remembered him as one of those he had seen in the residence in Québec. The boy he did not know. As the Jesuit steered past him, Casson looked at the priest's hand on the paddle. The index finger was severed at the joint. Casson's paddlers saw it too.

"Iroquois," one said to the man behind him.

Shit, Casson thought. Now they will leave us. We'll be stuck here on the river with no paddlers and a fucking fortune in pelts.

He looked at the Jesuit's sickly face and monkish

beard and felt a flush of anger. And then, as though to irritate him further, the Jesuit smiled at him and called in his hoarse voice, "It must have been Saint Joseph who sent you to us today."

Saint Joseph my ass, Casson thought, but he forced a smile. The fucking Jesuits were the real rulers of this country. Champlain was completely under their thumb. He was like a priest himself, now, in his old age, lecturing everybody else on the importance of saving the Savages' immortal souls.

When the canoes had all been pulled clear of the water, Vallier said to the boy, "What happened to you?"

The boy looked at Vallier as though he did not understand.

"What happened?" Vallier said, again.

"We're starving," the boy said.

"There's some cooked sagamité in our kettles," Vallier told him and asked his paddlers to bring it up.

While they waited for the sagamité, the priest, the boy and the girl stood silent as animals, and when the kettle was placed near them they went at once to it, scooping up handfuls of the cold greasy sagamité and stuffing it into their mouths. But, after their first swallows, they ate slowly, in the manner of starving people, as though the act of eating was difficult for them.

"How long are you without food?" Vallier asked.

"Eight days," the boy said.

The Savage girl, eating, suddenly vomited on the ground. Still retching, she went back to the kettle and scooped up another handful of the sagamité. As she did, Casson's lead paddler came up to her. "What happened?" he said in the Algonkian tongue.

"Shut up," Casson said, in sudden rage, going to the girl as though he would hit her. He turned wildly, staring at the priest. "Don't tell them what happened," he said. "If we lose these paddlers we'll never get back to Québec."

The priest, masticating slowly, nodded, to show he understood, but at that moment Vallier's head paddler came up to the girl and said, "Was it Iroquois?"

"You shut up," Casson said again, turning back to the girl, raising his hand as though he would strike her. But as he did, the French boy, thin, bruised, wild-eyed, pulled a hunting knife from his belt and held it against Casson's cheek. "Are you fucking crazy?" Casson said to him.

"Wait," the priest said, coming forward, holding up his hands. "Are we all mad? You have saved our lives. Daniel, put away that knife."

"You tell her to keep her mouth shut, do you hear?" Casson said. "Vallier! Help me."

But as he spoke he saw that four of his paddlers had come up behind him. He felt them at his back, as though their hatchets might strike into his skull. He turned around, but they were not armed. Then, their leader, Karatisich, ignoring him, walked up to the Savage girl and said, in Algonkian, "Why are you with these hairy pigs? Are you their prisoner?"

"No." She pointed to the French boy. "He is my betrothed."

"And where are your people?"

"In the winter hunting place below the rapids."

"You came from there?"

"Look, Karatisich," Casson said, going between him

and the girl. "We will give these people food and help, but we must leave at once. I have promised you extra presents if we reach Québec before the snows."

Karatisich pretended not to hear him. He looked at the girl. "Were your people killed?" he asked.

"Shut up," Casson screamed at the girl. He knew he had lost control, but he could not help it.

"Be quiet," Karatisich said to him, then told the girl, "Pay no attention to this hairy fool. What happened?"

"Iroquois," she said. "Below the rapids. They killed my mother and ate my small brother before our eyes. My father died eight days ago."

"How did you get away?"

"They took us to their village and began to caress us. They would have gone on until, at last, they burned and ate us. But on the first morning I killed the guard and we ran away."

"Is that true?" Vallier said to the priest, his eyes staring in fear. "Cannibals?"

The priest nodded. Vallier turned to Casson. "What are we going to do?"

"We go on, for Christ's sake," Casson shouted hysterically. "Come on, you've heard enough. Let's get them back in the canoes."

"We can give you a ten-day supply of sagamité," Vallier said to the priest. "That will take you through the upper lake and the small river to the inland sea. You will meet the Allumette on the upper lake. We will give you trade goods. You can have the Allumette guide you to the great lake."

"If you make a receipt, I will sign it," the priest said.

"Our Superior will repay you in Québec. But, of course, there is no repayment for your kindness."

"Get the sagamité," Casson was shouting to his paddlers. "Bring the dried sagamité, now. Hurry."

"It will be dangerous," the priest said to Vallier. "But remember, you must travel at night. That was our mistake. The Iroquois do not hunt at night. Now, tell me. You have been in the Huron country?"

"We just came from there," Vallier said.

"Did you see any of our fathers?"

Vallier nodded. "We spoke with Father Brabant in Ossossané less than a month ago."

"Then he is alive?"

"He is alive, but one of the priests in the villages was killed," Vallier said. "It seems there is a sickness in many villages. The Savages haven't had this illness before, and they blame it on a sorcery of the Jesuits."

"Who was the priest who was killed?"

"Come on," Casson said, coming up. "Make out that paper and let's go."

"Wait a minute," Vallier said. He sat on a log and began to write out a receipt. "Who was the priest Father Brabant said was killed?" he asked Casson. "I don't remember his name, do you?"

"Of course I don't remember," Casson said, in great irritation.

"He was in one of the northern villages," Vallier told the priest.

"Ihonatiria?" the priest asked.

"Yes, that's right, that was the name."

The boy, who had been listening, came up to Vallier. "Why did they kill him?"

"I don't know. Father Brabant wasn't able to get up

there. He was told of the killing by one of the Christian Savages." Vallier stopped. "Are you the priest they sent to replace him?"

"Yes."

"I wouldn't go there now, if I were you. Go to Ossossané and see Father Brabant first."

"But Ossossané is several days south of Ihonatiria," the priest said. "Isn't that so?"

"Six or seven days' paddling," Vallier said. "But what does that matter, if your life is at stake?"

"For Christ's sake, give me that goddamned receipt," Casson said. "You just sit there talking."

The priest turned to him. "My son," he said, in his hoarse voice. "Please, do not blaspheme."

"I am not of your faith," Casson said rudely and began to scribble the receipt.

"Father," said Vallier. "We are going into danger. Will you hear my confession?"

The priest at once went to him, putting his arm on Vallier's shoulder. Together they walked off toward the trees. Casson, finishing the receipt, watched in disgust as Vallier knelt and the priest, sitting on a rock, made the sign of the cross.

Casson saw that his paddlers were watching. He turned to the French boy. "Fuck it," he said. "Have they no sense? The fucking Savages think it's some sorcery against them. Kneeling and making those signs. Shit!"

But the French boy, ignoring this, asked, "What is this sickness up there in the Huron country? Do you know?"

"Fever." Casson looked at the Savage girl, who had come up and now stood near them. "Does the priest allow you to sleep with her?" he asked.

"Fuck you," the boy said. "Tell me. Are there Iroquois where we are going?"

"There are Iroquois in the Huron country, yes." Casson said. "They are killing the Hurons and driving them out." He looked over at the priest and Vallier. "Shit, what's keeping them? How many sins has he got to tell?"

"They won't be long," the boy said. He turned to the girl and said in Algonkian, "Are you still sick? Is it better now that you have eaten?"

"It's better," she said.

Vallier and the priest returned. Casson handed over the receipt and the priest signed it. "I cannot tell you how grateful we are," he said. "When you reach Québec, will you tell Father Bourque that you saw us and that we are well?"

"*If* we get to Québec," Casson said. He called to the leader of his paddlers. "Karatisich? We are ready."

Karatisich stood, flexed his arms as though he had a cramp and then came over to Casson. He smiled and said, "We are going on, then. But we are all agreed. I have spoken to the others. We will not go below the rapids."

"You have been paid to go to Three Rivers," Casson said. "Are you a bunch of pissing women, then?" He laughed to show he was not giving offense.

"Will you protect us from the fucking Iroquois?" Karatisich asked. He, too, laughed to show he was not angry. "I think not. You Normans kill beavers, not warriors."

"We will travel at night," Vallier said. "There is no danger at night."

"What do you know about the danger?" Karatisich asked. "I told you. We will not go below the rapids." He walked away and called to the other paddlers. "I have told them. We will go now."

The four fur-laden canoes were put back in the water. The paddlers took their places as Casson and Vallier walked down to join them. The priest, the boy and the Savage girl stood beside the sacks of dried sagamité they had been given. "Thank you, and God bless you," the priest called.

▼

As the canoes moved out into the main current, the traders turned to wave their fur caps in the air in a gesture of farewell. Impelled by the downrushing flow of the river, their craft skimmed at great speed over the water and, in less than a minute, had disappeared from sight.

Daniel, watching from the riverbank, his hand on Annuka's shoulder, thought, What if those are the last Frenchmen we will ever see? He looked around him. The river was again that desolate place of swirling currents, sudden winds and the strange creaking of the trees which lined the shore. A chill November dew covered the ground. He turned to her. Although she had just been physically sick, although her face was still discolored from the beatings she had suffered, he felt a familiar rush of joy. He looked into her brilliant dark eyes and, as always, saw there the self she had not given, that unpredictable Savage self, which judged him by rules and signs he did not understand. He looked down at the bags of sagamité. In six days we can reach the inland sea where the Hurons live. There we can marry. If my hand heals I can become a hunter. If not, I can live as the Hurons do by growing crops. But then, as though the man still stood beside him, he heard the voice of the trader. "Fever."

He turned to Laforgue. "Father, if there is fever in Ihonatiria, should we not go first to Ossossané and consult with Father Brabant?"

"I have been ordered to Ihonatiria," Laforgue said.

"He said one of the priests is dead."

"All the more reason to go there first."

"Tell me," Daniel said. "Do you ever have doubts?"

"About what?" The priest picked up the bags of sagamité and began to walk down to the canoes.

"About this journey."

"Yes, I have doubts," the priest said. "Now more than ever."

"Tell me about them," Daniel said.

The priest smiled. "It's better not to. Instead, look at this food. And these trade goods. We could say that God did not forsake us today."

And suddenly, as though to confirm his words, they hard Annuka call, "Look, look!"

Around a bend of the river came two canoes. In the canoes were Savages, paddling. The Savage in the lead canoe rose and made a sign of greeting.

"Allumette," Annuka said. "They will guide us." She began to wave. The Allumette leader waved back. His canoes moved toward the shore.

▼

The Allumette controlled the Mattawa River. The following day, having been paid in advance by the trade goods in Laforgue's possession, they brought them to the Mattawa and, paddling relentlessly, reached the portage known to the French as La Vase, a twisting snake of river, mired in mud, through which the canoes must be dragged and carried. After an exhausting day in this maze, they reached Lake Nipissing. Heavy winds caused high waves as the Allumette led the priest's canoe across the fourteen miles of lake and into the small river described in Father Brabant's instructions. Here the canoes glided under high rocky banks in a two-day journey which ended when the Allumette leader pointed ahead, and, from the dark green color of the river, the canoes emerged into the clear waters of the great bay. From there, having said their farewells to their Allumette guides, and aided by prevailing winds, they rode the waves down the shore of the lake. At night they camped under pines which grew on barren orange-colored rocks. They rose each day just before dawn, while frost still covered the ground. It was a race, and they knew it. Until the midmorning sun warmed them, they paddled, their hands freezing, their shoulders wet with a penetrating dew. They ate sparingly, a mouthful of cold sagamité on starting, and cooked sagamité when they lit their nightly fire. On the fourth day, Laforgue, anxiously watching each configuration in the bay against the map he had been given, pointed to an inlet fed by a small river. "There," he said. "We go there."

"Are you sure?" Daniel asked.

"From the map, it seems right."

Annuka, staring at the shoreline, pointed. There, on

the riverbank, was the remains of a small fire. "Huron," she said.

They landed. Annuka seemed nervous. She inspected the fire and said it was two days old. A chill wind turned to rain, and, although it was early afternoon, they built a shelter and lit a fire. "We are less than a day from Ihonatiria," Laforgue told Daniel.

"What did he say?"

"He said we are less than one day from the village," Daniel told her.

"Then tomorrow he must go on alone."

"We have only one canoe."

"He still must go on alone. You and I will come on foot."

"But that could take three days."

"He must enter the village alone."

"Well, we can go with him and wait outside the village."

"No." Suddenly she was angry. "You go with him and you destroy the prophecy. Don't be so stupid, Iwanchou. We will go on foot. In two nights we will reach the village. Nicanis will be there before us. And the dream will be obeyed."

"Daniel," Laforgue said. "Don't argue now. We have come this far together. Maybe she's right. I will take you upriver and, at noon, you can disembark. I will go on alone."

But the next morning when, as usual, they woke just before first light, Annuka would not get into the canoe. And so, waving a farewell, Laforgue, alone, paddled up the small river which led to the village of Ihonatiria.

As he rounded a bend and was gone, suddenly, An-nuka began to tremble. Daniel put his arms around her but she pulled free. "What's wrong?" he said.

She shook her head, refusing to answer, then squatted on the ground near the dying fire. With a shiver of apprehension, he saw that she had adopted the posture of Chomina, head down, arms folded across her chest.

"Why do you sit like that?"

"Be quiet," she said. "They are all around us now. Their day is ending as ours begins."

"Who?"

"The dead. There are many here. There has been a sickness."

TWO

$\mathcal{T}$he mirror, oval in shape and encased in a wooden frame, had been dropped last year by one of the Savage children whom he had taken as a pupil. Now it was cracked in a spider web of tiny sections, which split and altered his image as he moved in front of it. Reflected, the face which examined him from the web of slivered glass seemed the work of an indifferent caricaturist who had tinted his beard gray, enlarged and discolored his right eye and drawn the left side of his face in a lopsided, lifeless manner, the mouth's corner turned up in a stiff rictus which parodied a grin.

He looked in the mirror through no motive of fear or hope, or even of disgust. He studied the left side of his face as his brain issued the simple commands of speech. Speech came, but he was not sure that the sounds could be comprehended. With his good right arm, he steadied himself on the makeshift crutch and then, with great care, dragged himself through to the second room of this longhouse, which he and Father René Duval had partitioned off in sections to form the residence of the Jesuit mission of Ihonatiria.

The second room had been their kitchen and workroom and a classroom for the children they had taught. Now, its kettles and pans, its tables and rough benches seemed like exhibits in some museum of former times. Water which had leaked in under the loose doorjamb covered this part of the floor with a thin film of ice, making it necessary for him to hammer and crack it before he trusted his moribund body on its treacherous sheen. He moved to the large wooden chest in which the corn biscuit was stored. Each day he ate biscuit and drank water which was now bad-tasting, lying in a pail covered with a film of dead midges. He gave thanks before he ate, saying the words he had always said. When he had finished he sat for a long time, half listening for Joseph's footstep. But Joseph, whom he had christened as the first of his converts—even Joseph no longer came. It was as Joseph had predicted. No one would come any more into this house. The village waited for his death.

Today, straining to hear sounds, he thought of former days when he had striven for silence. The residence had been built inside the palisades erected by the village to protect the community against enemies, but he had asked that it be placed as far as possible from the other dwellings. He had asked this so that he and Father Duval would have quiet for their devotions and studies. He had not known until the fever came that, like so many of his requests, the Savages interpreted this as hostile behavior. The Savages distrusted privacy. In time of illness, noise and company were thought essential to drive out evil spirits. When the fever had first come upon him and then on Father Duval, the villagers had crowded in with advice, beating drums and offering ritual cures. He turned them away and asked for silence. It was a fever of a sort he had known in France, a fever brought on by a sudden chill. After fourteen days he was rid of it, and Father Duval, being younger and stronger, threw it off in half that time.

Then the fever spread. Unluckily, the first to die was a young woman who last year had refused their efforts to convert her. Her family said it was the Blackrobes' revenge. Since then more than thirty men, women and children had caught it and perished. At first, the village did not believe the young woman's family, and he and Father Duval had been welcome as they went about dispensing herbs and other simple medicament from their pharmacy. They were welcome because the Savages knew that they had thrown off the fever. No one else had done so. Therefore they must be sorcerers of strength. But at that time, he and Father Duval, seeking to baptize those who were about to die, had said in all innocence that baptism would lead their souls to heaven. The Savages reacted with alarm. They had hoped that baptism would cure the fever. Now, they said, the Blackrobes did not promise a cure but performed an act which led to the sick person's death.

That decision on the part of the Savages caused a

council meeting. It took place, he thought, on the week when he suffered his second and crippling stroke. But he could not be sure. No, it must have been later than that. Yes, he remembered clearly the day he heard drums outside the residence and, on going to ask the cause, found Father Duval's body, his head split by an ax, thrown into the doorway. He had carried Father Duval into the small chapel, which was partitioned off next to the kitchen. It was as he laid the body down before the altar that he fell and lost consciousness. And woke to the bad paralysis on his left side. How long ago was that? He was not sure. If the stench from the chapel was any guide, it was many weeks ago. The smell had been dreadful for a while, but now it was much less pungent. He had dragged himself into the chapel several times. The host was still in the tabernacle. Christ was present and watched over poor Father Duval's remains.

On the day after his stroke, he had managed, with a makeshift crutch, to go outside the residence. All hid from him. He called out, asking for someone to come and help him bury his dead. But no one came. A week later, Taretandé, the leader of the village, came with the senior men to visit him and told him that the warrior who had killed Father Duval had, next day, been stricken with the fever and had died. It was proof, Taretandé said, that the cure of the sickness lay in the Jesuits' hands. Taretandé asked him to forgive the village for the death of Father Duval. As a sign of his forgiveness, they asked him to lift the fever. When he told them there was nothing to forgive and that the fever was the will of God, they withdrew at once. Later, Joseph, coming to him under the cover of darkness, told him that the council had ordered that no one cross his path. It was said that he willed the death of the village but that their own sorcerers had striken him with the falling sickness and soon he would die. Meantime, the people waited. In his death they saw their deliverance.

Now, when he had finished his biscuit, he felt for his crutch and cautiously propped himself up, preparing to make the difficult journey across the kitchen to the chapel. He did not enter the chapel but, as usual, sat himself down just outside the doorway. From there he could see the statuette of the Virgin, which sat on a niche to the left of the altar. He could also see the tabernacle. The squeaking sound below the altar was the sound of mice. He prayed, as every morning, for the soul of Father Duval, a soul which did not need his prayers, he was sure, for Father Duval must now sit at the right hand of God in heaven, the first martyr of the Ihonatiria mission.

When he had finished his prayers, he allowed himself to think of Paris. He had been born forty-four years before in the Rue Saint Jacques, and now the Seine, the Île de la Cité, the markets of the Marais, the nave of the church of Saint-Germain-des-Près where as a boy he had dedicated his life to God, the streets, the sounds, the hawkers, the feast-day processions all paraded once again across the retina of his mind. Sometimes he heard the music of Palestrina played on his mother's spinet. And sometimes he saw his father's body, covered in black velvet, carried high on a bier through the crowded gravestones of the Cemetery of the Innocents to be buried with pomp and circumstance in the place where his father's father lay. At other times, as in a dream, he saw a grave marker in the Order's cemetery at Rheims, a marker which bore his name and this year's date: *Fernand Jerome, S.J., 1591-1635.* The stone marker was worn with age and greened with moss. A certain peace entered his reverie when he looked on this marker, evidence that he had lived and died. For in this emptiness, now that René Duval was dead, it was the aloneness of his fate which caused him, at night, to fall into a trembling as though his fever had returned. The Savages, once so noisy, were totally silent. Had they abandoned the village? Had they taken their dead and dying and moved to some other place? Perhaps he was surrounded by empty dwellings. Winter was at hand. Without a fire, he would perish of the cold.

But today, as he dozed in his accustomed place facing the small simple tabernacle on the altar which contained the body and blood of his Savior, he fancied that, in his reverie, someone called his name.

"Father Jerome? Father Jerome?"

It was a fancy, he was sure. The Savages did not use his French name. They called him Andehoua. But again, clearly, he seemed to hear it.

"Father Jerome?"

Stumbling, he hoisted himself up on his crutch and, warning himself to patience, began the careful trajectory toward the doorway of the residence. Again he heard his name. And then the voice, in French, called, "Father Duval? Are you there?"

▼

On either side of Laforgue the dwellings seemed deserted, but wisps of smoke from the openings in the roofs of the habitations warned him that he was being watched. Occasionally a dog ran up to sniff at him, and twice he saw children peering at him from the skin-covered doorways, before some hand plucked them inside. He had left his canoe at the landing place. Some twenty other canoes were beached there. He walked on. He had almost covered the entire area enclosed by the palisades when he saw, ahead, a longhouse, built like the others but with a wooden doorway and, on its roof, a small wooden cross. At once, approaching it in excitement, he called out, "Father Jerome? Father Jerome?" There was no answer. He quickened his pace, going up to the door, his heart hammering in anxiety. "Father Jerome?"

He tried the latch. The doorway was not locked. Surely this must be the residence? He opened and peered in. "Father Duval? Are you there?" Inside, he was met by a foul charnel-house smell which made him gag. In the darkness of the interior, there moved, unsteadily, a tall bulky figure. It spoke in a voice like the hollow echo in a sea cave. "Are you . . . ?" it said. "Are you there? Do I really see you?"

▼

Taretandé and Sangwati were in the fields when the messenger arrived. "A Blackrobe has come. He wears a long cloak and carries *raquettes* on his back. He has been beaten and his right hand lacks a finger. He came alone in a canoe."

"Where is he now?"

"He walked through the village. No one greeted him. He called out in the Norman tongue and all hid from him. He went to the Blackrobe's longhouse. He entered. Then I came here."

"And Ondesson, where is Ondesson?"

"I think they went to hunt."

"Find him," Taretandé said. "We must call the council. Join us by the river in the meeting place."

When the messenger had gone, Taretandé looked at Sangwati. They were brothers, born of the same mother, and did not need to hide fear from each other.

"If another one has come, and alone, it is not natural," Taretandé said.

"They are sorcerers," said Sangwati.

"More than sorcerers, they are witches. They are not men but evil spirits."

"You were the one who said we should not kill Andehoua but let him be, as he is dying of the falling sickness."

"I know," said Taretandé. "Ondesson will hold it against me. He would have killed him as the other Blackrobe was killed. One hatchet stroke."

"But even if you had killed Andehoua," Sangwati said. "Who's to say this other fucker would not have come?"

"You are right," said Taretandé. "They are not men but evil spirits. What can we do against them?"

They had been working with ten other men and boys in the fields, but now they took their leave and went to join the council members in the meeting place. It was a clearing in the woods not far from the village. When Taretandé and his brother arrived, Ondesson and the seven other council members were already assembled. All had been told the news.

Ondesson was the war chief. In the past he had deferred to Taretandé, who was chief in council. But today it was as though Ondesson had prepared a war party and was ready to set out. As Taretandé and his brother entered the circle, Ondesson said, "There is one solution. Both Blackrobes must be killed."

"But, fuck it," said Sononkhianconc, who was the leading sorcerer of the village. "You kill one, another springs up. And remember that Otreouti, who killed the first one, himself sickened and died within three nights."

"We will not kill them with a hatchet," Ondesson said. "We will caress them until they scream and are filled with fear. We will tell them how many of our people they have killed with their sorcerers' sickness and why we must pay them with death. We will cut our necks and let their warm blood flow into our veins, so that we gain their powers. We will eat the fuckers' hearts as soon as they have died. We will cut off their heads, their hands and their feet."

"And when will we do this thing?" asked Sangwati.

"Now."

"And what if, like the warrior who killed the other Blackrobe, we sicken tomorrow, all of us die within three nights?" asked Taretandé. "For these are not men but evil spirits."

"They are men, fuck it," said Ondesson in a loud, warlike voice. "They will bleed like men and die like squealing hares. If you are afraid to come with us, then sit and shit yourself."

"I ask a vote," Taretandé said. "I am the council chief. We will have a vote. Who votes for death?"

Eight hands were raised. Then Sangwati, Tare-tandé's brother, raised his hand also.

"Well?" said Ondesson. "Are you with us?"

Taretandé raised his hand. "Yes," he said. "And as council leader it is I who will enter their stinking long-house and tell them their fate."

▼

"And how many days have you been alone?" Laforgue asked, when the older priest had finished.

Father Jerome did not answer. "First," he said, "you know what must be done."

"No, Father."

"The body is the temple of the Holy Ghost. That must be your first task."

"The body is in the chapel?" Laforgue asked.

"Yes. By the altar. Those are now the remains of a martyr of the Church."

Laforgue stared at the pale paralyzed face, the en-larged discolored eye, the heavy gray beard. He thought of a painting he had seen in the cathedral in Salamanca, a saint's face but with a look of madness.

"Day and night, I have wondered how I could inter his remains," the sick priest said. "So let that be your first task. Afterward, you must find the leaders of the village. You speak the Huron tongue?"

"Yes. Not as you do, but I have studied it for two years."

"We must speak with them once more. We must convince them that this fever is not our doing. The Sav-ages are under the spell of their sorcerers. And the sor-cerers speak against us. Now, go. You will find a shovel and an ax in the outer room. The floor of the chapel is of earth. We cannot have a coffin, but we can bury him in God's presence. When you have dug the grave and interred him, call me. I will say the prayers for the dead."

Laforgue rose and went to the outer room. The stench was less overpowering there. He took a shovel and an ax and went into the chapel. As he crossed the threshold he made the sign of the cross and genuflected to the altar. As he rose from his knees he saw, sprawled beneath the tabernacle, the corpse of Father Duval, an arm thrown out as in a grotesque gesture of welcome. The face was already in a state of putrescence.

He looked away, then forced himself to look again. This was, as Father Jerome had said, the body of a Christian martyr. He saw the matted hair, the skull split by a hatchet, the dried blood and congealed fluids. Quickly, he picked a burial place and began to hack at the earthen floor. He threw off his cloak and unbuttoned his cassock and, in the dreadful stench, working like a man possessed, within an hour he had dug a rough trench, six feet long by three feet wide. He went to the corpse and, taking it by the heels, dragged it toward the grave. As he did, to his horror he saw the head, already split, come apart at the base of the skull as though it would separate into two halves. But then, with a lurch, he pulled the body into the trench. He stood, panting, and wiped his brow with the cuff of his robe. As he did, he heard a sound behind him.

A Savage watched him from the doorway. The Savage wore a long beaver cloak over a tunic and leggings of deerskin. His face was painted black on one side, red on the other, and his hair, elaborately arranged, was cut short on the one side and fell in a long braid on the other. Around his neck he wore a ruff of feathers, and bead bracelets decorated both of his arms. He carried no weapon.

"Come with me, sorcerer," the Savage said. "And be quiet." He spoke in the Huron tongue. He beckoned, and Laforgue followed him out into the kitchen of the residence. There, Father Jerome stood, tottering on his makeshift crutch. "Take his arm," the Savage said to Laforgue. "Help him."

Laforgue went to the sick priest's assistance and together, slowly, they made their way to the front door of the residence. The door was open, and outside they could see several Savage men, painted and wearing robes of ceremony. The Savage who had come to fetch them signaled to these men.

"He is Taretandé," Father Jerome said, in French. "He is their leader."

The Savages at once surrounded the two priests. Drums began to beat. Men and women, children and dogs came suddenly from all the longhouses, in a din of noise and excitement. Yelling and screaming they marched with the priests toward the largest longhouse, the place of assembly.

Laforgue, half carrying the sick priest, made slow progress in the din. When they entered the longhouse, he felt the paralyzed body sag and become almost a dead weight. He looked at Father Jerome. The priest seemed to have fainted. "Father Jerome?"

The sick man rallied and opened his eyes. In the uproar Laforgue could not make out the words formed by the half-paralyzed mouth. He leaned toward the priest's lips and heard, "Did you—did you bury him?"

"It's begun," Laforgue said. "I will finish later."

Ahead, a tall, heavily built Savage stood with three others, painted for war. All three carried heavy clubs.

"Ondesson," said the sick priest, nodding to this Savage. "Ondesson, we must speak together."

"Shut your hairy face," the Savage said, and laughed. "Are we all assembled?"

A roar went up from the crowd. People scrambled up on the sleeping platforms as though taking their seats at a performance. Laforgue, remembering that other time of torture, in the longhouse of the Iroquois, felt himself tense. Was this a parley, or was it what he feared?

"Come! You!" shouted Ondesson, beckoning to Taretandé, the council leader. "Tell them."

Taretandé bowed to the war leader, as though in thanks, then turned to face Laforgue and Jerome.

"Fifty-three are dead," he said. "Men, women, children. Fifty-three you have killed, of our people. And every night more sicken and die. No one lives once this fever comes upon them. No one who is a man like other men." He pointed to Jerome. "But *you* lived. You and the other witch. Both of you had the fever and lived." He turned to the crowd. "Today, I went into their longhouse. I went into that place, shut off, where they keep pieces of a corpse in a little box, a corpse they brought from France. And what did I find? This new one, this new witch who came alone to this place, was there, digging in the ground. And in the place where this fuckpot dug, there were the guts and head and body of the one we killed. He was hiding him under the ground so that some new fucking spell can be made."

There was a silence; then, suddenly, men and women began to moan and cry as in pain or terror.

"These are not men," Taretandé said. "They are witches. They must be killed as a witch is killed."

A roar went up. Father Jerome raised his crutch, waving it as though asking permission to speak. But as he did, Ondesson, the war chief, banged suddenly on the ground with his club. "They are men and they will die like men! We will caress them. We will take strips of their flesh, roast it on the flames and make them eat it. We will remove their fingers, one by one. We will cut out their hearts and give their bowels to the dogs. We will cut off their heads and their hands and their feet."

"Wait!" Father Jerome managed, despite his hoarse paralyzed speech, to make the word sound clear above the din. At once, the yelling ceased. "You must not do this," the sick priest shouted. "If you do, God will punish you! Do you hear me? God will punish you!"

"Prepare the coals," said Ondesson. "We will start with the coals."

At that, the din began again, rising to pandemonium. Three women ran to the fires and scooped up hot coals on birch-bark platters. They presented the coals to Ondesson.

"Strip the prisoners," he commanded.

At that, two warriors ran up to the priests. As they began to pull at the cassocks, ripping the buttons, the light died in the longhouse as though someone had blown out a candle. All looked up at the openings in the roofs and saw a sky black as night. Inside, only the burning beds of coals dimly lit the faces and figures of those near to it. In the darkness, the crowd, like some great panting animal, fell silent in dreadful unease.

Laforgue turned to Father Jerome. "What is happening?" he whispered.

"Come," said the sick priest, as, jacking his crutch under his armpit, he hobbled toward the doorway of the longhouse. In the dim light of the fires, faces moved away, letting them pass. They walked slowly out into the village street and looked up. And as they did, the eclipse moved, the sun gradually reappearing from behind its circle of blackness. "It is an act of God," Father Jerome said hoarsely. "Our Lord has saved us. Blessed be Thy Name."

An eclipse of the sun, an act of God. Laforgue, looking up as the light returned to the heavens, knew that, indeed, this must be God's hand. But somehow no words of thanks came to his mind, no prayer of gratitude passed his lips. Could this be, like thunder and lightning, an accident of nature, which had happened at this hour? Of course not. But still he felt no sense of miracle. He turned. The Savages were now pouring out of the longhouse, staring up at the sky. Laforgue looked at Father Jerome. The sick priest's discolored right eye was bright with a strange luminescence.

"Father Paul," the sick priest said, "God has given us this grace, this opportunity. Now, we must use it for His glory."

"In what way, Father?"

"You will see," Father Jerome said. He called out, "Ondesson? Taretandé?"

The leaders came forward, unease plain as speech on their faces.

"You have seen," the sick priest said. "God—our God—has warned you. How dare you try to injure us, who are God's servants? We are going back now to our house to bury our dead. You have seen the hand of God. You must change your ways. If you do not, we cannot help you. That is all I have to say." He turned to Laforgue. "Come, Father Paul. Let us go back to the residence."

Laforgue took his arm. Slowly, they moved away, the crutch hitting like a slow drumbeat as the sick priest hauled himself over stony ground. The Savages stood, looking to their leaders. After a few moments, Taretandé made a sign. The villagers began to disperse.

▼

"*Deus qui inter apostolicos sacerdos familium tuum. . . .*" Father Jerome, his paralyzed bulk looming over the small altar, began to recite aloud the prayer for a priest deceased. As he spoke he looked down at Father Duval's replacement, who knelt by the freshly covered grave. Soon the men of the village council would return. He knew what he would say to them. This would be his final task: to reap a great harvest of souls.

Laforgue, listening to the Latin, stole a look at the sick man who recited the prayer. He thought of the rotting corpse beneath the ground and in his mind saw the skulls of saints long dead, venerated in sanctuaries as holy relics.

Is this the martyrdom, the glorious end I once desired with all my heart and all my soul? Why have I ceased to pray? What error has come upon me so that, today, that eclipse of the sun seemed to me a phenomenon which, were I to believe in it as the hand of God, would leave me in the same murk of superstition as the Savages themselves? I should ask Father Jerome to hear my confession. I should tell him my doubts and ask for absolution. But if I do, this holy man who is close to death will know I am utterly unfit to take his place.

When night came, Laforgue settled the ailing Jerome on his pallet and then, still sickened by the stench in the residence, went outside and stood looking at the Savage dwellings. He heard drumbeats and the cries of sorcerers, trying to drive out the evil spirits which they believed to be lodged in the bodies of the sick. Dogs barked. Above him the sky was clear and cold and filled with stars. The Savages have not yet come to kill us. If they do not come, then this will be my home. When Father Jerome dies I will be in charge here, my life's work to convert these Savages now dying of a fever against which they have no defense. The Savages will not come to kill me. God did not choose me to be a martyr. He knows I am unworthy of that fate.

12

There had been no fever in Taretandé's house. But on the morning after the black sun darkened the sky, he woke to find that his new wife had begun to shiver and sweat. He rose at once and went to a sorcerer. But when he entered the sorcerer's house, the sorcerer's child was sick and a curing ritual was in progress. He went out and, walking through the village, heard drums and lamentations. He passed the hated longhouse where the Blackrobes were and saw their sign of crossed sticks on the roof. He remembered that the Blackrobes, in former days, made that sign with their hands and tried to teach it to the children. He remembered that, last spring, the Blackrobes had invited families with children into their longhouse and there had given the children presents of beads if the children would learn answers to questions which the Blackrobes taught about their god. He remembered that Aenons had warned that the Blackrobes did not speak of curing rituals to combat sickness, but of death and another life to which they wished to lead the people.

The Blackrobes spoke this way because they were the sorcerers of death. He thought of the black sun, which warned of their power. His new wife would die. Perhaps all of the people would die. Already, there was little fishing; the crops had rotted in some fields for want of harvesting. It had been a mistake to kill the first Blackrobe, for another had come alone, like a manitou, to replace him. The Blackrobes were devils of great power. We must treat with these fuckers. We have no choice.

It was as though, that morning, every man in the council had been touched by the same thought. Ondesson's son had shown signs of fever. Achisantaete's mother, who had had the fever four days, died during the night. Ondesson asked for a meeting.

"We must go to the Blackrobes," Ondesson said. "We must ask their help for a curing ritual to end this sickness. We must find out what it is that these sorcerers wish."

"The water sorcery for all of us," said Sononkhianconc. "That is what they will ask. And the water sorcery kills, just as the fever kills. They wish our deaths so that they can lead us into some fucking Norman place of the dead as their captives."

But Sononkhianconc was a sorcerer, and the council

members knew that, as such, he was jealous of all other sorcerers.

"That could be," said Taretandé. "But at least let us speak with them."

It was decided. The council members walked through the village, watched by all. They went to the longhouse of the Blackrobes and Taretandé entered there. A few minutes later he came out with the old Blackrobe Andehoua, who had the falling sickness and walked with a stick. Behind them was the stranger Blackrobe, who had been found with the corpse of the dead one, performing some evil spell.

In the longhouse of the council, all sat. Tobacco was offered but, although it was the first time the council had invited them to a parley, the Blackrobes behaved not as normal men but as enemies. They said they did not smoke.

When he heard this, Taretandé laid aside his pipe. "I understand why you will not smoke with us," he said. "We did you a great wrong by killing one of you. Now we are willing to give many presents to right that wrong. Tell us what things you want from us."

He waited. "We do not take presents," the old Blackrobe said.

Taretandé felt himself begin to sweat. Had these sorcerers decided on death for all? Was there no talking to them? "We have come to you today because we are all agreed that you have the power to stop the fever. You are its masters. The village is dying and the sickness spreads. We now put ourselves in your hands. What must we do for you so that you will perform the curing ritual that will rid us of this sickness?"

As he spoke, he saw the old Blackrobe turn and whisper to the other one. Then the old Blackrobe raised his stick, signaling that he would speak. Taretandé bowed to him.

The sick old voice rose in a quaver of anger. "Yesterday, the sun went black. You have seen the hand of God, our God who is above us, who is the only Lord of heaven and earth. What must you do that you will be cured of this fever? You must serve our God, who is your God. If you will end this contagion, you must make a vow to do His will. Do you understand?"

"No," said Taretandé, and smiled, hoping by a joke to turn away wrath. "We don't understand because we are stupid cunts. You must tell us what you wish us to do."

"Very well," said the old Blackrobe. "You must make a public vow that if God ends this contagion, you will be baptized and keep His commandments."

"The water sorcery?" asked Sangwati. "For all?"

"Yes," said the Blackrobe.

"And what does your god command besides the water sorcery?"

"You must give up those practices which offend Him. You must not cast off your wives, but keep them for life. You must not eat human flesh. You must not attend curing rituals or feasts of gluttony in which you become sick with eating. Above all, you must give up your belief in dreams."

"But how can we do that?" asked a council member. "The dream tells us what to do."

"You will have no need of dreams to tell you right from wrong," the old Blackrobe said. "Our Lord will tell you. I have not long to live, but this priest of God who sits beside me will take my place and live among you. He will give you God's orders. Now, you must go back to your people and tell them what we have said. All must be baptized. And I wish this to happen soon. Until you come before me for baptism, the contagion will continue."

Aenons, who was aged and of great intelligence, now signaled that he wished to talk.

"We cannot do these things," Aenons said. He looked at the older Blackrobe. "Andehoua, I thought of you as my friend. But fuck it, don't you see? If we do these things and if we give up our belief in the dream, then the Huron life, the way we have always known, will end for us."

"You will have no need of your former life," the Blackrobe said. "You will have a new life, as Christians. You will worship the true God and forget these childish notions which now fill your heads. When you die you will go to paradise."

"I want to live, not to die," said Ondesson. "And I do not want to have a wife like a burden on my back when I no longer wish to live with her. You are Normans. Your ways are not our ways. Why do you not respect that we serve different gods and that we cannot live as you do?"

"Can we not agree to take the water sorcery and still retain our ways?" asked Aenons. "If your god wants that, then we will work among our people so that all will take the water and be cured."

"Baptism is not a cure for the fever. It is not a cure for the body, but for the soul," the old Blackrobe said.

"Is it something, then, for our deaths, not for saving life?" asked Taretandé, and looked at the others.

"Yes," said the Blackrobe. "It will lead you to paradise, as I have said. But it may also help with the fever. For, if you do God's will, you may hope for his mercy. We will pray, night and day to God, asking him to take this sickness from you."

There was silence. Taretandé rose. Sweat ran down his face. "We will leave now," he said. The others rose also. They walked past the Blackrobes and out into the day. They went toward Ondesson's house. As they walked, they did not speak.

▼

When the two priests returned to their residence it was almost noon. Laforgue settled Father Jerome on his pallet and, with him, recited the prayers of the Angelus. Then he went into the kitchen and made a broth of corn husks. As the broth simmered on the fire, Laforgue began to scrub the kitchen and clear it of dirt. When they had eaten he went into the chapel and cleaned and scoured the altar, replacing the rough altar cloth. He opened the tabernacle and saw a chalice and hosts within. When he had finished his work in the chapel, he went back to the sick man, who seemed to be asleep. But as Laforgue began to sweep the floor of the room, Father Jerome groaned and turned on his side.

"Are you all right, Father?"

"I have pains in my chest. Soon you will have to dig another grave."

"Don't say such things." Laforgue came to him and

propped him up. "You are needed here. The Savages respect you."

The sick priest winced in pain. "Only God knows what the Savages think," he said. "And we are waiting for their decision. In either case, I welcome it."

"What do you mean, Father?"

"Today, or tomorrow, they will come back," Father Jerome said. "Either they will give us a great harvest of souls or they will put us to death."

"A harvest of souls?"

"The baptisms."

"Tell me," Laforgue said. "What if we baptize them and they then die of fever? Those who survive will turn against us."

The sick priest smiled, a smile which, because of his paralyzed face, was strange as a gargoyle's pout. "Those who die baptized will go to heaven," he said. "As for the fever, you and I must pray tonight. We must ask God to spare them. If it is His will, the fever will leave them and we will have many Christians here."

"Father, that troubles me," Laforgue said. "Surely, if they now ask for baptism, it will only be because they fear to die?"

"Or because they fear God," the sick priest said. "Alas, most Christians do not perform their duties because they love God, but because they fear Him. This fever is God's hand."

Laforgue looked at the paralyzed face. "God's hand?"

"Yes, yes! The fever is the tool given us to harvest these souls. If they ask for baptism, we must have a great public ceremony. And at once!"

"But surely it is our duty to instruct them in the Faith before we ask them to accept it?" Laforgue said.

"Of course! But we must not delay the baptisms." The sick priest's voice rose, almost to a shout. "Besides, it is permitted to baptize people without instruction if they are in danger of death. As are these people, Father. This sickness is killing them!"

"I am not easy with that thinking," Laforgue said. "It seems sophistic."

"It is not! The means are fair, if the end is good!"

▼

That night in the village Annieouton, a sorcerer, performed a healing ritual with drum, shouting and dancing, on a young woman who was ill of fever. By morning, the young woman's fever had left her. The sorcerer at once spread about this news, claiming that he had cured her. But that morning, also for the first time, two other victims of the fever suddenly ceased to sweat and shake and woke, their brows cool, their bodies weak but cured. Both were Huron men who had become Christians some months before.

These events were discussed at noon in a meeting of the village council. Sononkhianconc, the leading sorcerer of Ihonatiria, claimed that his fellow sorcerer had effected a cure and that there was no longer need of the Blackrobes. But the council disagreed. It was pointed out that Annieouton had performed this ritual a dozen times in the past weeks and that all his other sufferers had died despite it.

"It is the Blackrobes who have done this," Tare-tandé said. "Why did it happen last night when it has never happened before? They have done it to prove to us again that we are in their power."

"But why was the fever lifted from the young woman while a sorcerer was present?"

"Perhaps they did it to mock our ways," said Tare-tandé. "I know one fucking thing. Annieouton's beating drums did not hurt. But it did not cure the woman. We must treat with these witches. My wife is dying. I want her to live."

The council then voted. It was agreed to assemble the village. Even those who tended the sick were asked to come. The council did not propose a referendum. It voted to inform the village of its decision and to ask for all to cooperate.

"Of course there will be some who will not take the water sorcery," said old Aenons. "I, for one, will not give up the dream."

"But, listen, you silly old prick," said Taretandé, trying to joke him out of it. "Why give up the dream? We will do as they say. We will take the water. Then we will see what we will do."

"If we make vows to give up the dream, to keep our wives, to let our enemies die an easy death and all the other stupid demands the Blackrobes make, it will be the end of us," Aenons said. "If we make the vows we must keep them. For, if their god is strong as they say, then he will know if we lie to him."

"It will be the end of us if we die of fever," Ondesson said.

"Then I will die of fever," Aenons said.

On the second night of their journey toward Ihonatiria, Annuka and Daniel, lying in a makeshift shelter, woke shivering with the cold. A heavy frost covered the ground, and at dawn they rose and continued on their journey. About an hour later, Annuka saw a path in the forest which told her they were close to a Huron settlement. She stopped, looked at Daniel and said, "Come here."

He had already, many times, plucked out most of his boyish beard to please her, but now she pulled at his chin and face until he groaned and slapped her away.

"Wait," she said. She took off his cap. She braided and arranged his hair in the Algonkian manner, then, taking out the purse of skins in which she stored her necklaces, she painted his face brown on the left side and blue on the right. She took away from him his woolen cap and his French breeches and left him dressed much in the manner of an Algonkian warrior.

"When we go in there," she said, "we will not ask for Nicanis. We will act as though we know nothing of him, until we discover what has become of him. Remember, you are my husband, and Algonkin. We have been lost and separated from our people, and we wish to stay for a time with these Hurons."

"And will they believe that I am not a Norman?" Daniel said, laughing.

She looked at him and smiled. "Don't you know, you fool? You have killed the Norman in you. Now you belong to me."

When Laforgue awoke on his third morning in Ihona-tiria, he heard noise and shouting outside. He went to the door of the residence and, in the streets, saw many people going in and out of each other's houses, talking and arguing. The drumbeats of curing rituals had ceased. Laforgue went back into the kitchen and took some meal, crumbling it into a porridge for Father Jerome's breakfast. But when he went to see the sick man, Jerome had fallen off his pallet and lay helpless on the floor. "My other leg," the sick priest said, in an almost unintelligible moan. "I have no feeling."

Laforgue lifted him with difficulty and placed him on his pallet.

"You heard the noise outside?" the sick man asked.

"Yes, Father."

The sick priest caught his breath and rested for a moment. Then said, "If they bow their heads at sight of us, when they come here, it means they will kill us. Promise me . . ." He began to gasp.

"Yes, Father, what?"

"If we die, let us die with the name of Jesus on our lips."

"Yes, Father."

"And if it is the baptisms, let us perform them together."

"But will you be able to do that?"

"God will give me strength," Jerome said. "Listen."

Outside there was a great shout, then silence.

"Help me up," the sick priest said. "I will stand by the door." But he collapsed when set on his feet. "Very well. Put me down. Go to the door and wait. They will be coming soon."

Laforgue went through the residence and opened the wooden door. Outside, people stood in the streets, looking at him. Then, from one of the longhouses, three men appeared. They were Taretandé, the council chief, Ondesson, the war chief, and the sorcerer Sononkhianconc.

They walked toward him in silence. Laforgue waited. Would they bow their heads?

When they were within ten paces of him, they stopped. "Where is Andehoua?" asked Taretandé.

"He is inside."

"We want to speak to him."

"Come in, then," Laforgue said. "He cannot walk."

The three leaders entered the residence and followed Laforgue to the room where the sick priest lay. Cold sweat lent a silver sheen to his brow. His breathing was labored.

"We have decided," Taretandé said. "We will obey your god. Not all in the village are agreed, but the greatest number wish it."

"How many?" asked the sick priest.

"More than a hundred. And there are some who now say they do not wish it, but who will change when others in their family accept it. Besides, the cures of last night will make a difference."

The sick priest glanced at Laforgue. "God has seen fit to cure some of them," he said, in French.

He looked again at Taretandé.

"Do the people know what they must do? One wife, no human flesh, no curing rituals, the dream, all of it?"

"Yes," said Ondesson. "We told them! We've done every fucking thing you asked. Now, let's have the water. People are dying!"

"First, we must instruct those who will be baptized," Laforgue told Taretandé. "You must know who our God is and how you must serve him."

"There is no time for that," the sick priest said hoarsely. "We must do it now."

"You are right, Andehoua," Ondesson said. "We will do it today."

"Very well," said the sick priest. "We will start by baptizing those who are already ill with the fever. Assemble them outside this house. When we have finished, we will go on to those who do not have fever. First, the children. Then the others."

"I want to ask a question," said Sononkhianconc, the sorcerer. "Will those who do not take the water die of fever?"

"That is for God, not me, to decide," Father Jerome said.

"That is not an answer," Sononkhianconc said. "I have promised some of our people that I will ask you this question. Fuck it, I want an answer! Will they die?"

"I told you, I don't know," Father Jerome said. "But let me ask you. If you were our God, who would you spare? Your friend or your enemy?"

"*That* is an answer," said Sononkhianconc.

"Well," said Ondesson. "Let us get ready. First we will bring those who are ill of fever."

When the leaders had left the residence, Father Jerome told Laforgue, "When the time comes, let me be carried outside. We will need a kettle filled with water.

We will baptize them one by one. Father, think of the joy of this day."

"I will get the kettle," Laforgue said. He went into the kitchen and, taking a cooking kettle, went out to the village well, which was close by a small river that wound around the edge of the village. As he walked through the village, he was aware of eyes on every side. People fell back at his approach and children ran inside the dwellings. For the first time in his life, he knew what it must feel like to be feared. When he reached the well, two women, washing clothes nearby, moved away at sight of him. He filled the kettle, and as he did a woman's voice whispered, "Nicanis?"

He turned, astonished. Standing by the palisades was Annuka and a young man. At first, he did not realize that this young man, a beardless painted Savage, was Daniel.

"What have you done?" he said to Daniel, surprised.

"Please don't speak French," Daniel said. "What has happened? What is this assembly?"

"The village is going to be baptized. Why are you dressed like a Savage?"

"We were not sure if you were alive," Annuka said. "It's safer like this."

"They say you cured three sick people in the night," Daniel told him. "Is that why they are asking to be baptized?"

"Yes," Laforgue said. Suddenly, to his surprise, he began to weep.

"What's wrong, Father?" Daniel asked.

"If everyone is taking the water, I will take it too,"

Annuka said. She looked at Daniel. "And then we can marry."

"Father?" Daniel turned to Laforgue. "What do you say? Will you marry us?"

"Yes, yes," Laforgue said, wiping his eyes. "But I must go now." He walked away, carrying the water-filled kettle. Daniel has become a Savage. And I, what am I? Do I still have the right to challenge Jerome, who is strong in his faith, I who am an empty shell?

As he approached the residence he heard shouts and saw a young man running, pursued by two warriors armed with clubs. One of the warriors was Sangwati, the brother of the council leader. The warriors gained on their quarry and felled him about two hundred yards from the residence. They then looked back at Laforgue, who, alarmed, ran into the residence. He put down his kettle. "Father Jerome?"

There was no answer. He ran into the sick priest's room. On his knees, his shoulder leaning against the edge of a table, was Father Jerome. But as Laforgue came closer he saw that the body had been propped up against the table leg, and that a hatchet had split the head at the base of the skull.

As Laforgue stared at this sickening sight, he heard footsteps behind him. He turned, in panic, expecting a hatchet blow. Ondesson and two other Savages came into the room. They carried hatchets.

"Wait," Ondesson said to the other Savages. He approached and looked down at the dead man. "The one who did this will not trouble you further," he said. "And if any others seek to injure you, we will protect you. Shit! Why didn't we remember that there are some in this village who have become mad with fear? I am sorry.

We are all sorry. You mustn't think we are your enemies."

"I don't think that," Laforgue said.

"Then you will cure us? We are bringing the sick
up now."

"The sick?" Laforgue said. He looked back at the
dead priest. "Wait," he said. "I must think."

"Don't turn against us," Ondesson said. "I am asking you. Help us. We will obey your God."

"I must think!" Laforgue said. "Leave me."

There was a silence. Then Ondesson signaled to the
other painted faces. All three went out through the
kitchen and into the street. The wooden door was left
open. In the quiet which followed their departure, Laforgue heard a faint buzzing noise and saw that flies had
settled on the dead priest's face. With his hand he
brushed them away. I must bury him. I will bury him
beside Father Duval. I will ask Daniel to help me. I must
pray for his soul.

But as he looked at the blood-clotted face and dead
eyes, his mind stumbled again into thoughts of despair.
What are these baptisms but a mockery of all the days of
my belief, of all the teachings of the Church, of all the
saintly stories we have read of saving barbarians for
Christ? Why did Chomina die and go to outer darkness
when this priest, fanatic for a harvest of souls, will pass
through the portals of heaven, a saint and martyr? What
is my duty now, if not to follow the dictates of my conscience and refuse them baptism until they truly accept
and worship Our Lord?

He turned and walked through the silent house into
the dusty chapel, still sickly sweet with the smell of pu-
trefaction. On the altar rested the small wooden box with

a golden cross which contained the body and blood of Christ; beside it, the statuette of the Virgin, brought from France, painted in garish colors of pink, white and blue. He looked at the empty eyes of the statuette as though, in them, some hint might be given him of that mystery which is the silence of God. But the statuette was wooden, carved by men. The hosts in the tabernacle were bread, dubbed the body of Christ in a ritual strange as any performed by these Savages. God, whose wishes he had dedicated his life to fulfill, was, in this land of darkness, as distant as the pomp and magnificence of the Church in Rome. Here in this humble foolish chapel, rude as a child's drawing, a wooden box and a painted statuette could not restore his faith. Yet somehow he must try.

He knelt. He made the sign of the cross and then, as though he had never said the words before, he began to recite. *"I believe in God, the Father Almighty, Creator of heaven and earth, and in Jesus Christ, his only Son, Our Lord, Who was conceived of the Holy Ghost, born of the Virgin Mary, suffered—"*

He did not finish. Someone stood behind him. He turned and saw an old Savage in the doorway. "What are you saying in your tongue?" the Savage asked.

"I am speaking to my God."

"Is that little spirit there your god?" the old Savage said, pointing to the statuette.

"No."

"I am Aenons," the Savage said. "Shit, man, I was a good friend to Andehoua, and it grieves me that he was killed. But listen, Blackrobe. I am speaking against you today. You and your god do not suit our people. Your ways are not our ways. If we adopt them we will be neither Norman nor Huron. And soon our enemies will know our weakness and wipe us from the earth."

Laforgue did not answer. The old Savage turned and walked to the doorway of the residence. Laforgue saw him go out into the street where, already, the sick had been carried up to be baptized. He watched the old man move among the sick and their relatives, urging them to return to their homes. And as he stood in the doorway, a dozen men and women who had been sitting just outside the residence got up and came to him. One of them greeted him. "Father, we are the Christians here. We want to thank you for healing two of our family last night and for lifting the fever from three others today. Everyone has seen what you have done. That is why they come here now. Everyone knows we were right to worship Jesus. We thank you, Father."

"Three more were cured today?" Laforgue asked.

"Yes, yes, as you know. Tell me. Is it true that Andehoua was killed by a hatchet?"

"Yes."

"Then must we pray for him?"

Laforgue, unable to speak, nodded. He saw two other men join Aenons and go about shouting warnings. He heard them say again that, as Christians, the Huron people would lose their way and be destroyed. He turned and closed the door. He sat at the table and tried to still the sudden trembling of his body. Outside, the shouting increased. The door of the residence was pushed open. Silhouetted against the light he saw Taretandé, the council chief.

"May I enter?"

Laforgue rose. "Yes, come in."

The council leader walked into the kitchen and

looked around as though afraid. He went to the doorway of the dead priest's room and stared at the kneeling figure. "Does this grieve you?" he said.

"Why do you ask?"

"Because there are some who say that you Blackrobes are not men but witches. And witches feel no grief."

"We are men," Laforgue said.

"Who can believe you? What sort of men are you? You don't come here, as other Normans do, to trade for furs. You ask to live with us in our villages, and yet you stay apart in this house. No one may sleep here and you hide your nakedness from us. Why? If you are men why do you not fuck women? Why do you keep a corpse in that room and eat it to give you strength? Why did you bring this sickness which was never seen here before? And why do you use it to kill us, if we refuse to bow down to your god?"

"We do not use it to kill you."

"No. The dead one, in there, Andehoua, didn't he tell us what we must do? That we must give up our ways? Well, we have told our people and they are agreed. We will do what you want, all the things you asked. All of them. That is what I came to tell you. We are ready. Baptize us."

"No," Laforgue said.

Taretandé sat down heavily at the table, facing Laforgue. "Why? Because we killed Andehoua?"

"No."

"Then why do you want us to die?"

"I do not want you to die."

"But without the water sorcery we will die."

"I didn't say that." Laforgue put his head in his

hands and sat for a long moment, in silence. "The water sorcery will not cure you."

"Then what *will* cure us? Last night and this morning some have been cured. That is your doing, isn't it? Well, isn't it! Fuck it! Answer me!"

"It's not my doing," Laforgue said.

"Then why did it happen today? Why?"

There was a silence. "It—it was the will of God," Laforgue said.

"Your god?"

"Yes."

"Then we are ready," Taretandé said. "Our people are waiting. You say you are a man and not a witch, and I believe you. I ask you now, are you our enemy?"

"No."

"Do you love us?"

"Yes."

"Then baptize us."

The council leader rose and went out of the house. In the street, the murmuring of the crowd grew louder. Laforgue got up and went into the chapel. He looked again at the blank eyes of the statuette and thought of the prayer half finished on his lips when Aenons came. Had that statement of belief in God any more meaning than Taretandé's promise to do God's will? What *was* God's will? He looked at the tabernacle. He felt the silence.

Do you love us?

Yes.

He went to the chest in which vestments were stored and took out a linen alb, pulling the long white smocklike garment over his black cassock. He took up a gold-embroidered stole and, from habit, touched his lips to it before putting it around his neck. He walked past the dead priest, going to the door.

Outside, a cold wind came from the great lake. Before him, huddled in the village street, were four rows of litters containing the sick. Behind them stood the children of the village, and behind the children were the men and women not yet stricken by fever. He saw, standing to his right, Taretandé and Ondesson, with the other members of the council. And, close by, he saw Daniel and Annuka. He signaled to Daniel, who came up at once.

"Take the kettle," Laforgue said. "Help me."

He faced the crowd. Slowly, he raised his fingers, making the sign of the cross, touching his brow, his chest, his right shoulder, then his left. All watched this sorcery. Then, with Daniel carrying the kettle, he went down to the first row of the sick. He took a small ladle from the kettle's rim, filled it and poured a trickle of water on a woman's fevered brow, saying in the Huron tongue, "I baptize you in the name of the Father, and of the Son, and of the Holy Spirit." The Savage woman stared up at him, sick, uncomprehending. He moved on, saying over and over the words to make them Christians and forgive their sins. Was this the will of God? Was this true baptism or a mockery? Would these children of darkness ever enter heaven?

He looked up at the sky. Soon, winter snows would cover this vast, empty land. Here, among these Savages, he would spend his life. He poured water on a sick brow, saying again the words of salvation. And a prayer came to him, a true prayer at last. *Spare them. Spare them, O Lord.*

Do you love us?

Yes.